Praise for *Brenda If You*

MW00982170

Wry humour, keen observation ~~and memorable characters make Torsten~~ sten Schoeneberg's writing unforgettable. You'll laugh and be left wanting more.

JEREMY LOVEDAY,
Victoria City Councillor, Founder and Director
of the Victorious Voices Youth Arts Festival
and spoken word poet

Brenda Craigdarroch is likely a relative of Anne Shirley (of Green Gables fame): a witty philosopher, a naïve daydreamer and a bit of a brat. Brenda does not have adventures in the world; rather, she is an adventure that happens *to* the world. I would like to sit down with her for tea and conversation about her views on stinging insects and lost objects and snooping through strangers' houses — partially because she is such an intriguing character and partially because I want to punch her.

Torsten Schoeneberg's narrative poetry flows as easily as warm conversation: thought-provoking, relatable, punctuated with surprising moments of laughter. This collection is a delight to both read and listen to, and is recommended for reading aloud amongst friends over tea or wine and witty banter.

SUSAN CORMIER,
Producer, Vancouver Story Slam
and The Short Story Show podcast

Brenda Craigdarroch Doesn't Care If You Read This Book but I did and found the whimsy of it startling and humourous, not in a laughing-out-loud way, but in a way that Brenda would deeply appreciate, a kind of slightly odd interior chuckle at irony and happenstance at memory and forgetting.

Torsten Schoeneberg offers this curious and wonderful collection of stories in verse form steeped in observations about life and things ordinary from an unusual vantage. Brenda sees the world her own way. Fun to read and worth pondering, even if like Brenda, you don't believe and are always right.

DANIEL SCOTT,
Artistic Director, Planet Earth Poetry

BRENDA CRAIGDARROCH DOESN'T CARE IF YOU READ THIS BOOK

BRENDA CRAIGDARROCH DOESN'T CARE IF YOU READ THIS BOOK

TORSTEN SCHOENEBERG

THREE OCEAN PRESS

Library and Archives Canada Cataloguing in Publication

Title: Brenda Craigdarroch doesn't care if you read this book / Torsten Schoeneberg.
Names: Schoeneberg, Torsten, 1983- author.
Identifiers: Canadiana (print) 20200306952 | Canadiana (ebook) 20200306995 | ISBN 9781988915234   (softcover) | ISBN 9781988915289 (EPUB)
Subjects: LCGFT: Humorous fiction.
Classification: LCC PR9110.9.S36 B74 2020 | DDC 823/.92—dc23

Editor: Kyle Hawke
Proofreader: PJ Perdue
Cover and Book Designer: PJ Perdue

Three Ocean Press
8168 Riel Place
Vancouver, BC, V5S 4B3
778.321.0636
info@threeoceanpress.com
www.threeoceanpress.com

First publication, September 2020

*Thanks to my wife and daughter
for accepting Brenda
as part of our extended family*

Acknowledgements

The texts in this volume were performed at various open mics starting in 2017 in and around Victoria, BC, on the traditional territory of Lkwungen nations, also known as the Songhees, Esquimalt and W̱SÁNEĆ peoples.

Thanks to all the hosts, participants and audiences of:

Tongues of Fire	Speak, Easy
The Word Congress	Planet Earth Poetry
Spotlight: Prose Open Mic	Open Mic Night Brentwood Bay

Thanks also to the venues for these series and their hardworking staff:

Caffè Fantastico	Village Empourium
The Mint	Hillside Coffee and Tea

I want to acknowledge Paul Shortt's Ocean Mic and Springboard Open Stage, as well as The Rabbit Hole, which were the first shows in Canada where I read from my writings. These shows did not live to meet Brenda, but without them, she might never have been born.

Also, many thanks to the Vancouver Story Slam (and its offspring, the Short Story Show podcast), organized by Susan Cormier and Bryant Ross and facilitated by the staff at Hood 29, who have introduced Brenda to a very welcoming audience on the mainland.

A chapbook with earlier versions of ten of these stories appeared in 2018. Shout-out to everyone who got a copy: Hold on to it, it might become a collector's item. Not least because it contained little vignettes by Irma Rodenhuis, whose support in this and many other things has been invaluable.

Said chapbook also benefited hugely from help by Kyle Hawke, who since then has worked unremittingly to publish this book. Beyond this, his enthusiasm for subtleties of word order, punctuation and line breaks made him a congenial editor. Paradise would be a place where we could discuss all these things without time pressure.

Contents

Brenda Craigdarroch
Never Believed Them

Brenda Craigdarroch never believed them.
When they sang songs about the glory of God, in churches,
   before Christmas, in perfect harmony,
she did not believe them.
When they posted their philosophical whimsies on Facebook,
with witty political asides,
making use of evolutionary theories
to demonstrate that their latest life decision makes perfect sense
   in what they called a "global context,"
she did not believe them.
When they told her that her morning would be
a *happier* morning
if she had bought that specific brand of coffee,
she did not believe them.
She might drink that specific brand of coffee anyway.

Not believing them was, from a very young age, one of Brenda's habits.
She did it quite regularly,
often several times a day.
While sitting on the bus, she did not believe them;
when she was chopping garlic, she did not believe them;
in particular, she did not believe them when she was having a shower;
sometimes she strongly not believed them in the middle of a movie,
or while collecting chestnuts,
or at the hardware store she used to frequent
   on the first Monday

of each month,
where she occasionally — not often, but occasionally — stopped in the
    middle of an aisle and paused for a few seconds,
during which she did not believe them,
before she resumed her shopping activities for water-resistant caulk
and metal screws:
flat-head, pan-head, oval-head, hex-washer-head both slotted and
    unslotted, zinc-plated.
Brenda liked to screw.

She tried to restrict her strongest fits of disbelief to times when
    she was by herself,
especially in the bathtub,
but every now and then a sort of panic possessed her,
that some person thought *that* she believed them
because she had not expressed her disbelief, nor acted it out,
and also,
even though Brenda by principle assumed
that all the others did not believe them either,
she could not be certain of that,
and the others might actually believe them.
The assumption that they believed them was not in
    apparent contradiction to most of their actions,
so maybe,
she thought,
actually everyone
except her
believed them:
she was the only one who persistently not believed them.

The ridiculousness of this thought got her over it,
usually.
Only three occasions are known wherein Brenda panicked enough
    to let loose
and forcefully expressed her disbelief to people around her:

One time, when her third boyfriend,
a programmer of Bengali descent

with Australian citizenship,
who was always surprised how much she seemed to enjoy sex,
asked her why she had not taken the garbage out,
she replied that she had been busy.
"Busy with what?" he asked.
"Not believing them!" she yelled,
and he accepted that and made tea.
They later broke up for reasons entirely unrelated.

One time, on a bus going up Johnson Street, after seeing a sign
    on a store wall,
she pulled the cord,
got off at the next stop, ran back in her boots,
positioned herself on the street a few metres in front of that sign
    which read
    "Our greens, proteins and supplements will help you live agelessly,"
tried to stop each and every car and, when successful, told the people
    therein what that sign was:
a fucking lie.

And one time, at the checkout of the hardware store,
where she had been waiting in line just a little too long,
she
somewhat unexpectedly
started to say
    "It is all not true! It is all not true!"
in a calm but strong, convinced, persuasive voice,
whereupon,
somewhat unexpectedly,
other people in line started nodding their heads, then gleefully began to
    join in, saying
    "It is all not true! It is all not true!"
getting into a kind of rhythm, chanting.
And even when Brenda had already gotten over her state,
the customers
as well as the clerks,
and an elderly couple who had come in from the street,
started to modulate certain tunes on the sentence

"It is all not true! It is all not true!"
going up and down the scale, using counterpoints,
elaborating the chant into more and more intricate melodies,
finally reaching a song of perfect harmony,
while Brenda quietly put her pack of
#8 Stainless Steel Pan-Head Phillips Sheet Metal Screw (5 Count)
on the counter
and did not believe them.

Brenda Craigdarroch
Once Gave a Jigsaw Puzzle

Brenda Craigdarroch once gave a jigsaw puzzle
of a Japanese painting
as a Christmas gift
to her fifth boyfriend,
a bitcoin miner from Winnipeg.

The bitcoin miner from Winnipeg loved Japanese culture.
He explained to Brenda, while putting together the edge of the puzzle,
how this drawing, and he pointed to the image on the box,
consisted of only 17 distinct brushstrokes and yet
showed a clearly discernible monkey staring at the reflection of
    the moon in a pond,
a composition which was of course open to various philosophical
    interpretations.
However,
the bitcoin miner from Winnipeg added,
what predominantly amazed him was the connection of
    simplicity and expression:
the simplicity of just 17 brushstrokes, expressing a clear but
    multi-valued image.
That is the quintessence of Japanese art,
    the bitcoin miner from Winnipeg explained to Brenda.
It takes long years of hard practice and training, the bitcoin miner said,
to achieve the ability to express
so much
with so little.

He said there were other drawings, made up of only
   10 or 11 brushstrokes,
which elucidate elaborate landscapes
with mountains,
rivers,
and cherry blossoms;
only 10 or 11 brushstrokes, thrown onto the canvas by a master
seemingly within a couple of minutes,
but based on years of exercise, meditation and preparation,
the bitcoin miner from Winnipeg said
as he was separating the puzzle pieces with grey parts
from those that were entirely white,
and Brenda was folding up some of the wrapping paper
   for possible reuse.
Then she started to help with those pieces that were entirely white.
The best method she came up with was testing each of them
   against each other,
seeing whether they fit.
This was in the old days,
when bitcoin mining was still feasible as a private business,
with some expensive but affordable special processors
whose cooling fans were quietly humming behind the Christmas tree.

After their third date, he had explained his bitcoin mining to her.
Then Brenda had read all she found about bitcoins on the internet
in one afternoon, and understood enough to see that
most questions asked on the bitcoin forums
were dumb,
and eventually bought five bitcoins from money
she originally had saved for Christmas presents.

   "There are drawings that consist of just four brushstrokes,"
the bitcoin miner from Winnipeg said.
   "Four brushstrokes,
     conjuring a detailed scene of rural life,
     with a farm and the fallow lands and wet meadows
     and several sheep.
     And a dog strolling at the riverbanks.

And through one window in the farmhouse, one can see
the family having tea.
Amazing craftsmanship. Amazing,"
the bitcoin miner from Winnipeg said.
Then he recounted that the artist who made that drawing
had lived in a monastery for 34 years,
taking a vow of silence
and eating nothing but three bowls of rice with raw vegetables a day
and fish on Fridays.
He had made his brush from a tree that had been grown
on the south side of a hill just outside the monastery boundaries,
planted 250 years ago for that exact purpose.
Eventually the tree was cut down in a spiritual ceremony,
the best part of it was made into a brush,
the best ink was prepared and the best canvas was prepared, and then
within 20 or 30 seconds or so
but after four days and nights in which the master stared, open-eyed,
    at the canvas,
he threw that magnificent rural scene on it
with the family in the farmhouse, and the sheep, and the dog,
and a flock of birds rising in front of Mount Fuji
with four brushstrokes.
   "That's fucking amazing, isn't it?"
the bitcoin miner from Winnipeg said.

Brenda had managed to connect patches of seven, four, three and
    another four pieces respectively.
Her boyfriend had finished the monkey and the reflection of the moon.
Some of the ripples on the pond were still in disarray.
She really liked him.

Months later, she was quite sad when he followed the path
    of cheaper electricity
and set off to work on a bitcoin mining farm in Mongolia.
From there, he wrote Brenda a letter
in which he enthused about the clear skies at his workplace,
and related to her that among the miners, after their shifts,
word went around about a painting,

7

made by a 97-year-old hermit
who lived in a tree in the Hokkaido highlands,
who on a canvas spun out of leaf fibres,
with ink made of the blood of a sacred frog
mixed with abandoned spider webs,
using his left little toe as a brush,
had drawn a painting of the forest he had lived in for the last 60 years,
as well as the sad love story which had turned him into a hermit
   60 years ago,
    in 48 panels,
     with two strokes.
Brenda folded the letter for possible reuse
and with part of the money in her bitcoin savings
bought a two-year supply of finest organic rice.

Brenda Craigdarroch
and the Philosophers

Brenda Craigdarroch once submitted an entry
to an essay writing contest
held by the Department of Philosophy
of the University of Northern British Columbia in Prince George.

She got invited to the award ceremony
albeit it was made clear in the invitation that she would receive only
an honourary award.
She drove up and sat down in an auditorium next to
a pale man in a tweed jacket.
The pale man in the tweed jacket was a professor of ethics
at the Saskatoon College of Trinity and Rye.
He was the winner of the contest
and told Brenda that he had been flown in, all expenses paid, by the
    philosophy department, which consisted of sixteen people who
    seemed to fill up the rest of the auditorium:
Eight people on the left side
men with black hair in grey suits
and women with blonde hair in blue blazers —
and eight people on the right side,
men and women in alpaca sweaters
with somehow unspecified hair colours.
The men in suits
and women in blazers
sat upright in their chairs,
several of them looking at their phones and tablets;

the men and women in alpaca sweaters were mostly hanging their limbs
    over their chairs,
one squatting on the floor,
and some of them playing with their genitals.

When the chair of the department, a blonde woman in a blue blazer,
    gave her speech,
the contest winner listened attentively,
the philosophers in alpaca sweaters hissed and rolled their eyes,
and the philosophers in suits and blazers applauded.
Her speech sounded as if she had recently taken a course in rhetoric
and was now using the occasion to try out some stylistic devices.

When the vice chair of the department, a man in an alpaca sweater,
    gave his speech,
the contest winner listened attentively,
the philosophers in suits and blazers showed each other stuff
    on their phones
    and giggled,
and the philosophers in alpaca sweaters said
    "Nice one!" and "Right on!"
His speech sounded as if he had read an article in the *Guardian*
    last night
or watched some John Oliver clip on YouTube
and was now using the occasion to recycle some witty bits from that.

What Brenda foremostly learned from the speeches was
that she must have had misunderstood the contest criteria,
and her essay
"How Numerology Upsets Me as a Spiritual Being"
had received an honourary award even though it did not address
    the actual topic of the contest,
which seemed to be something about identity politics, art
    and gardening.
She decided to consider *that* quite an honour, all the more
since she had composed most of it in her head
while being held awake
by the snoring of her second boyfriend

a poet from Portland
who referred to himself as 'The Verge'
in his waking hours.

While Brenda was waiting for the contest winner to give his speech,
The Verge was at her apartment, working on his epic
Mealybugs of California
which would get published sixteen months later as
The Mealybugs of California
with a definite article
to avoid confusion with a taxonomic standard work of the same title,
but without definite article.

In ignorance of these future events,
Brenda listened to the speech given by the contest winner,
the pale man in the tweed jacket,
which sounded as if he had put actual effort into it,
and wherefrom Brenda remembered the remark
  that
   "Asking questions is a good start, but pointless
    if one lacks the ability to assess answers"
which she used several months later,
in an argument with The Verge,
albeit in an entirely different context.

Brenda Craigdarroch
Would Not Stop Smoking

Brenda Craigdarroch would not stop smoking.
She did acknowledge that smoking was detrimental to her health,
but so is driving around in a car or eating steak,
and as she would not interfere when people did
  those things which she did not,
she saw herself having a rightful demand for non-interference
  regarding her tobacco habits.
Whenever a person told her to stop smoking, she invariably replied
  "Go fuck yourself"
or,
if that person happened to be from Seattle,
  "Go fuck yourself, asshole!"
If somebody tried to criticize her smoking
  via a suggestive question
    like
  "You know that smoking is bad for you, right?"
    or
  "Have you ever considered *quitting* cigarettes?"
she would always reply
  "Shut up, asshole."
However, if a person asked that last question
  in a tone of genuine interest,
without the implied suggestion to stop smoking, like
  "Have you *ever considered* quitting cigarettes?"
she replied with a sober
  "Considered, yes; decided against it"

or,
if that person happened to be from Seattle,
    "Considered, yes; decided against it, asshole."

Besides the actual joy that smoking a cigarette could give her,
a joy which faded a bit over the years, like with any hobby
    when it becomes a habit
and is done too often without real awareness and conscious presence,
she occasionally found it a very practical excuse to get out
    of a situation,
like if she had been having dinner at a Greek restaurant with
    her fourth boyfriend
and there was a party of 23 high school teachers taking up two-thirds
    of the room
and the five of them sitting closest to Brenda and her boyfriend
were sharing gossip
that made one of them cry out ecstatically,
Brenda would have, with mild complacency, taken the opportunity
    to leave the room and smoke a cigarette.

This one, smoked out in the cold next to a sign with fake Greek letters
and while several busses passed by,
she would smoke with an awareness and mindfulness
    which reminded her
how much she was no longer doing *any* thing with that much
    awareness and mindfulness
and she'd decide to come back in
to her boyfriend
in spite of the frolicking teachers,
and enjoy the rest of her stuffed eggplant,
the conversation,
and later at home the sex with her boyfriend
much more than she had enjoyed anything lately,
thanks to that one cigarette in the cold.

Brenda chose her places to eat partly by the criterion of how easy it was
    to get out and smoke there,
with the exception of a cake place and bakery downtown she

regularly frequented
even though its owner enforced a strict
— fair to say: militant —
anti-smoking policy in and around his establishment.
That owner was a German immigrant
who among his loyal customers, who all, including Brenda,
had a love-hate relationship with him,
was known as
'the cake nazi'.

Brenda fell in love-hate with the cake nazi on the day
when she was having some buttercream cake and suddenly heard
from across the room
    "Are you sure it's ze processed sugar zat
      makes you feel uncomfortabel at night
      or ze creeping realizashun zat your
      pseudoprogressive hedonist vestcoast lifestyle
      is just as meaningless as evrry uzzer kind of existence?
      Just asking."
Then and there, Brenda knew that she would come back to the place,
even though she was not allowed to smoke
    within ten metres of the building.
She felt that a gooseberry cream cake and a hot chocolate would
cushion her longing for a cigarette anyway and were also
    worthy of relishing
bite by bite
with clear consciousness.

At that bakery, there was always a bowl of apples on the counter
whose purpose was that,
if an uninitiated customer came in and ordered something like
    "A vegan blueberry muffin, please,"
the cake nazi could point at the bowl and say
    "Vant sumsing vegan? Eat an apple!"

Customers were actually free to take an apple.
There was an assortment of Fuji, Elstar, Braeburn,
Gala, Ambrosia, Kanzi,

Jonagold, Lady Alice, Spartan,
Boskoop, Honeycrisp and Golden Delicious;
and Brenda knew *all* the apples were delicious,
and so were the cakes,
which is why a sustaining group of patrons,
including Brenda,
kept coming to the place
and just sat through the occasional yelling one could hear
  from the counter, like:
    "You vant vat?!
      Dairy-free gluten-free cheesecake?!
      Zat's cheesecake vizout cheese and cake!
      Eat an apple!"

One day
four teenagers came in and ordered:
    "A pumpkin-spiced decaf latte with soy milk,"
    "A gluten-free oatmeal cookie, low-carb, no sugar,
      with carob chips,"
    "Can I have two-thirds of a banana loaf like that but made with rice
      flour, and some cashew butter on the side, but only with cashews
      in it, please make sure it's not mixed with sesame or sunflower
      seeds, and I cannot eat almonds either,"
    and
    "A piece of the strawberry cake, but without the crust if it
      contains eggs, and almond cream but make sure it's a non-
      GMO kind, and… do you have kombucha with coconut
      flavour?"

While the staff ushered the teenagers out
the cake nazi ordered the kitchen to close for the time being
then proclaimed that
    "Zis country is doomed!"
and went on a five-day hiatus.

Each of those five days,
Brenda stopped by the place,
observed a growing number of patrons lingering there,

waiting for it to re-open,
trading addresses of ersatz bakeries for the time being,
and exchanging the best insults they had heard from the cake nazi.
Rumour had it that after what was now called
   the "coconut kombucha incident"
he had locked himself up in a darkened room
with two of his own loaves of dark rye bread
and five gallons of water
reciting paragraphs of
   Schopenhauer, Nietzsche, Immanuel Kant and Hagenbuch
in order to, as he said,
"pyoorify" himself
and be able to bake again
    "viz nusing but bootter, flour, shugar, eks,
     and prrezence of ze mind."

And Brenda smoked a cigarette or two,
and invented some new curse words for the city of Seattle
which she abhorred and despised
without having a specified reason for that.

Brenda Craigdarroch's Keys

Each time Brenda Craigdarroch moved out of a place
— her father's home, the student dorm,
her sixth boyfriend's house, the apartment on Finlayson —
she always kept a little something that allowed her
to access the memories she had of that place:
A key.
A door key.
She kept actual door keys to those places.
And then sometimes she sneaked into them.

Whereas that was certainly normal and actually wished for
    by her father
when she moved out of his place at 17,
it was a bit unusual for the other places.
Brenda had made it a habit to make and keep
duplicate keys of every place she moved into,
starting with the student dorm,
and even did it for her girlfriend's condo
where she just stayed for two weeks between moves.
It gave her a feeling of safety:
It meant that even though one day she would leave the place,
she would not entirely leave it.

Of course, she was very careful not to disturb the new inhabitants
and always made sure they would not witness her coming in,
staying inside for a while,

and then leaving.
She was quite good at that.

She took firm precautions not to change
   any of the new inhabitants' arrangements,
not to move furniture or ornaments
or even dirty mugs standing around.
Instead, Brenda often singled out a certain spot in the place
which presumably was of no importance to the new owners,
nor had been of great importance to her when *she* had lived there,
but now had become special to her
because it had not changed,
or something about it had not changed,
and when Brenda was in that spot, she could most easily
   access the memories
of the entire place
and her life there.

In the student dorm, that was the toilet.
In her sixth boyfriend's house, it was a dusty corner
— far from the kitchen, on the right side of the couch —
which was not quite reached by the sunlight from the window
   across the room.
When she was in the neighbourhood and could fit in a visit
while her ex and his current girlfriend were both off to work,
Brenda sneaked in and squatted in that dusty corner for a few minutes,
and even though much of the furniture had changed,
from that perspective, the room looked most familiar to her,
and she could most easily see it
as it had been
when she had lived there.

In the apartment on Finlayson, it was the bedroom closet.
The three or four times Brenda sneaked in there
some months after she had moved out,
she rushed through the narrow hallway,
dodging the mirror,
and through the living room with the new paintings and chairs and

distastefully nonmatching colours,
and headed straight towards the bedroom closet
and hid in there,
quietly breathing in
the bedroom closet smell
which had stayed just the same.
Her hiding in there, in the dark,
was rather convenient one time because the new tenant,
a small round man whose breathing sounded like constant sighing,
had suddenly come home early,
and Brenda, not wanting to disturb him,
stayed in the closet for about two hours, until he took a shower,
which opportunity Brenda used to quietly sneak out.

It was surprising that few people ever changed their locks.

The key for the student dorm had had a very visible "do not duplicate"
    written in capital letters on it,
but she was known at her hardware store as one of the best customers,
and the young guy working there as locksmith pretended not to notice,
and instead knowingly smiled at her.

She was a bit taken aback when the lock to her sixth boyfriend's
    house had been changed,
apparently on the initiative of his new girlfriend.
So now she could *only* visit the place,
and for moments stand in the dusty corner beside the couch,
on the few occasions when she was actually invited to the house
for his birthday parties and, later, the baby shower.
She decided to not take it personally though —
maybe they were annoyed not by her,
but by somebody else who had lived there once.

Thinking about that, Brenda started to wonder
whether she, in turn,
was having visitors at the place where she was living right now.
She paid more attention to details
and after a while figured out

that there were at least two people semi-regularly visiting
    her apartment.
One who could not resist the urge to dust off an old vase,
which Brenda had found on a shelf when moving in,
and just left standing there,
which maybe had not even been theirs, but had now become
    special to *them*
because it was the one thing that had stayed exactly the same for them.
And one other person who came every Wednesday evening,
when she was out for her pottery class,
and took a bath in the bathtub.
Brenda liked the idea and deliberately stayed out longer after her class.

But eventually, some weeks later, when Brenda's pottery class was over
and she was home on Wednesday evenings,
the bather now came during the night between
    Tuesdays and Wednesdays,
usually from 2 to 3 am,
and tried very hard to let the water in as quietly as possible.
Brenda was usually asleep at that time anyway,
but when she was not,
she pretended not to notice,
and instead knowingly smiled into the dark.

Brenda Craigdarroch
in Buenos Aires

Brenda Craigdarroch dreamed about living in Buenos Aires.
Not metaphorically,
in the way that she would daydream about living there
on her bus commute,
or would have half-baked plans to move there
    after quitting enough jobs,
or would mention it as a place to be
to friends during conversations at housewarming parties,
but literally:
Every couple of weeks, in her sleep, she had dreams wherein
    she lived in Buenos Aires.
Which is remarkable because she had never been to Buenos Aires;
in fact, Brenda had never crossed the equator in her life
and had only a vague idea about what Buenos Aires looked like.
Accordingly, the cityscape she saw in her dreams looked
    rather like Florence,
which is also remarkable
because Brenda had never been to Florence either.

So in her dreams
Brenda would walk the dusty orange hills of Buenos Aires
in the hot sun
along the stinking river
avoiding the mopeds
now and then being held up by market people
who tried to sell her screensavers

or jigsaw puzzles with maps of Scotland on them,
speaking Italian,
while she could see the dome of the cathedral far off
in the hazy smog
of Buenos Aires.

In several dreams
she arrived on an airplane that landed in a gorge
between gigantic skyscrapers.
The airplane went down into the water,
and Brenda would get off
onto a beach which immediately turned into a lawn
   (with a decent slope)
where many people lay on towels and made love.
In some other dreams, she arrived by train
or rather on the subway
in the huge subway station that connected many of her dreams,
with one connection going to Vienna.
And two or three times, she just fell from the sky
and landed on a dusty grey hill with suburban houses,
and a view of downtown,
and a milk car going around,
and there were little garden patches
and cafeterias
and the Eiffel Tower
in Buenos Aires.

Then she would sit in a restaurant
with an astronomer and her English teacher from grade ten
and her English teacher would try to tell a joke, but Brenda would focus
   on the astronomer
mentioning that when she was a kid, she wanted to be
   an astronomer herself
to which the astronomer replied that
of course, all the cool kids want to be astronauts
but the nerdy ones want to be astronomers
and her English teacher still tried to tell a joke
in that colourful vegetarian restaurant

with servers dancing sirtáki
in Buenos Aires.

Or:
Brenda's family was having a hefty argument about
  some religious issue
out on the street, on a huge avenue actually.
The debate soon turned into a cake fight
when the Portuguese navy came in
with their nuclear-driven sailships
and reinforced the peace
in Buenos Aires.

Or:
The earth cracked open
and all sorts of flowers and plants came up, some of them carrying
Patagonia outdoor clothes as their fruits,
and somehow everybody just started to play golf,
  golf golf golf
said one of the car salesmen to Brenda,
and the head nurse asked
    what's the colour of golf?
    what's the temperature of courage?
    and does snow have corners?
To which Brenda replied with a warm honest smile
that stayed with her all through the jungle
and when the warm snowflakes came down
and she wrote her postcard,
she had a clear feeling that golf is blue
in Buenos Aires.

True, not much in her dreams was faithful to the real Buenos Aires,
but then again, even if it had been, Brenda would not have known.
Still
it was always clear, in the clear sense of dreams,
in the part of dreams where you just know something for a fact
without it being connected to what you see or sense,
you just know it

as if it had been put on one of the title cards in a silent film
that this was in Buenos Aires,
that *this was* Buenos Aires
and golf,
the sport golf,
the abstract concept of golf,
is blue.

Brenda Craigdarroch
and the Dishwasher

Ever since an unspecified traumatic event in her childhood,
Brenda Craigdarroch lived in irrational fear of dishwashers.
That was a strange but harmless condition
during the first years of her adult life
because she lived in places without dishwashers
and in the rare case that she
attended a party
and the whole party crowd moved to the kitchen
and the kitchen contained a dishwasher
she just pretended to have to poop
and locked herself up in the bathroom
occasionally checking whether at least one interesting person
had moved back from the kitchen
to the nice orange vintage sofa in the living room,
the dishwasher-free living room.

Also, Brenda was actually able to stay in the kitchen
for a few minutes;
her condition was not terribly bad.
She might even walk past the dishwasher
   and give it a playful punch,
which looked like one of the funny things *Brenda* would do
   in the eyes of her friends
like a weird thing *that person* would do in the eyes
   of the people who did not know her
but which, in or behind her own eyes,

was mostly a test of strength and an attempt to see
   if she had made progress
so that she might stay around dishwashers one day
and have
the *option*
of living a bourgeois life
with a house, a car, a husband, two children, a dog and a dishwasher,
and could stop pretending to have to poop so much.

Indeed, her condition seemed to improve over the years
which is why she made the decision
to move in with her sixth boyfriend
even though his kitchen incorporated a dishwasher.

It was unclear what, exactly, *was* her fear.
Was she afraid of some improbable but real possibility,
like the dishwasher breaking and leaking lots of water,
causing a huge mess and lengthy arguments
   with insurance agents and landladies?
Or did she fear the dishwasher could cause a short circuit
or suddenly explode —
an event which admittedly was *very* rare,
but according to her Google search *had happened*
at least three times in the US,
   once in Australia
   and once in Nigeria,
although the Australian article in particular was vague
   about the exact incident
and was hosted on a potentially unreliable news portal
whose other articles were concerned with an alien civilization living
   underground on Jupiter
and the havoc supposedly wreaked on businesses by the supposedly too
   liberal Australian refugee policy.

Or was Brenda afraid of something supernatural happening
like, when she walked into the kitchen at night,
the dishwasher would suddenly start to glow red
and speak to her in a growling and mocking voice

threatening to eat her
bathing in the power
a demonic kitchen appliance holds over a woman in pyjamas.

Brenda felt that all these possibilities were part of her fear
to some extent
although none of them, when followed through, rang entirely true.

Her boyfriend tried his best to be understanding
once he got over his insistence that Jupiter is a gas planet
therefore has no 'underground' where an alien civilization might dwell
  and fake climate change to make humanity easy prey by tricking it to
  give up industrialization.
But
his occasional jokes about himself being afraid of
  a poltergeist in the microwave,
although well-intended,
did not help Brenda.

Eventually, the issue resolved itself
as Brenda more and more lost her fear of the dishwasher,
or transferred it to issues whose fear garners more social acceptance
like termites, getting pregnant and lack of real estate.

Because of the pregnancy issue, she eventually broke up
  with that boyfriend
who found another woman with whom he soon had
  the kids he had wanted,
kids in whose eyes Brenda, who stayed on good terms
  with his new family,
would be Auntie Brenda,
as opposed to their real aunt Sherri, a nice lady who lived in
  a house in the Kootenays
with her husband, two children, two cars, a cat and an interest
  in Buddhism,
who one day slipped on some spilled dish soap in her kitchen
and fell flat, face-first, into the cutlery basket of her dishwasher.

Brenda Craigdarroch
and Social Media

Brenda Craigdarroch had the following approach to social media:
She had accounts on every single network, platform and sharing site
    known to her,
and spent a significant amount of time browsing through them,
following friends, acquaintances and people she followed
    for no reason known to her,
but Brenda would not contribute, share or post anything,
ever.

Actually, Brenda *used* to post, share and comment occasionally
until one day,
a friend of hers,
or rather a friend of her third boyfriend's,
shared an article about the Black Lives Matter campaign on Facebook
and wrote a few sentences about it
which led to some arguments being posted as comments
to which Brenda wanted to contribute a comment of her own,
wherefore she wrote three declarative sentences and one exclamation.
But before Brenda clicked 'post'
she read again what she had written.
Then she changed the word order in two of the sentences
    and added a fourth.
Then she read it to herself again
and replaced the exclamation with a different one.
Then she rephrased the final sentence,
and then

copied the whole comment out of the Facebook tab
   into a Word document
and went for lunch.

Over lunch, she forgot the whole thing,
but the next day when she browsed through her daily Facebook feed,
she remembered yesterday's Black Lives Matter discussion and opened
   the Word document.
She went on to check her boyfriend's friend's page,
where she had to scroll down to find yesterday's Black Lives Matter
   discussion,
because meanwhile, her boyfriend's friend had shared two articles
   on different issues
and a photo of the tacos he'd had last night.
When Brenda found yesterday's Black Lives Matter discussion,
the comment she had wanted to comment on had been commented on
   by two other people,
which had led the discussion in a slightly different direction.

So Brenda copied all comments so far
   into her Word document,
and spent 45 minutes writing a new comment,
which eventually boiled down to five sentences
with an implicit but no explicit exclamation.
She copied it
into the comment box in the Facebook tab
read it to herself again…
inserted a comma…
then felt that this time,
finally,
the entire discussion so far
and all former comments considered,
she was completely fine with what she had written
and deleted it.

This happened on impulse —
felt strange,
but gave her a peculiar feeling of satisfaction.

It felt good.
So good that she wanted to feel that again.

Ever since then, Brenda did it that way:
She wrote multi-paragraph comments on hotly debated topics
putting serious effort and considerable time into, say,
a differentiated view of the constitutional crisis in Brazil,
and when she felt absolutely sure about what she had written
and saw no way to further improve it,
she slowly let the mouse slip over the 'post' button…
and instead deleted the whole text and closed the tab.

She wrote some nice posts of her own, spending half-hours and hours
arranging sentences and pictures
and then did not post them,
got excited about political articles or music videos, copied the links
and then did not share them.
On various forums, from chemistry.stackexchange to the hardware store
    self-help site,
she wrote thoughtful answers in which she backed up
    each important claim
    with more than one source,
then marked the entire text and clicked 'cut'.

Over the months and years, Brenda wrote hundreds of tweets
which were not tweeted,
composed dozens of Facebook posts, funny, thoughtful or sad,
which were never posted.
One day, she had seven browser tabs,
    three Word documents
    and two picture editors open,
working on:
Her Instagram photo series "Rice Puffs: An Abomination";
Her deliberately unironic comment on the latest WatchMojo video
("Top 10 Cartoon Shows from the 1970s Which Do Not Feature
    Dragons");
and four tabs just to be able to put the comment
    "remember when we had true music, not the crap the industry

sells to young people today" simultaneously under
a) a Bob Dylan bootleg from 1967 of extraordinarily bad quality
b) a video of ABBA live in concert, 1979, Agnetha singing
   "Gimme Gimme Gimme"
c) a video of diverse Earth, nature and outer space footage set to Pink
   Floyd's *The Division Bell*
d) the 2015 updated music video of The Connells' one-hit wonder
   "'74-'75".
This fourfold simultaneous comment she almost *did* post
because she really wanted to know under which video she would get
   the most thumbs up,
but instead, she just rewatched all four videos, one after another,
and then closed all tabs without leaving a trace.

Over the years,
Brenda kept a Word document, titled 'internet drafts',
where her complete unpublished musings, essays and
   several photo albums were kept,
and all her unpublished comments, her
   "I really do not care about your beach holiday pictures,"
as well as her own beach holiday pictures, her
   "I like you, but could you stop posting your supposedly ironic
   self-centred trivialities,"
as well as her own (mildly ironic) self-centred trivialities, her
   "I agree with the intention behind this video but the main argument
   is flawed,
      hence it really does a bad service to a good cause,"
each of them with a link and a concise description of
what post, file, video or other content
posted by whom and on what date it referred to,
all combined in one big .doc file
which at one point had reached 237 pages and which
Brenda
ritually,
each year
on the evening of April 12th,
from the first to the last line,
deleted.

Brenda Craigdarroch
and Religions

Brenda Craigdarroch had the following approach to religions:
She tried to be a member of each and every religion known to her,
which was easy for some because you could be a member
　　by just believing yourself to be one in your head,
you did not have to sign up or register for anything;
whereas for others, you did have to register or sign up and pay
　　for a membership
or at least get ostracized if you didn't donate.
Which Brenda never did
so she was kicked out of many religions
but liked to stay in the ones that let her in
and never bothered her for just being there,
silently watching and listening but never responding,
never joining a chant,
never saying amen,
never signing up for next time.
And occasionally Brenda just went to
　　a temple, mosque, synagogue, church,
whatever building she found where some worshippers let her in
　　without asking too many questions,
then she attended a ceremony, quietly watching and listening
and not bothering anyone and not being bothered,
and feeling a little less lonely.
As a surprise to herself, her favourite were the Jehovah's Witnesses.

Brenda Craigdarroch
and the Biocapacitator

Brenda Craigdarroch got reasonably upset when she learned
that the federal government had seized
her and her neighbours' storage lockers
to build a biocapacitator
in the basement of their apartment building.
She had not seen that coming.
One day when she came riding home
and wanted to put her bike in the locker,
she found many yellow barrier tapes in the basement
with little stickers dangling from them, saying 'government property'
and a paper note on the wall to inform residents
    about the national interest in biocapacitators,
which gave the former owners of these lockers
a grace period of 72 hours to remove all their stuff.

Even though Brenda was not in principle against
    the building of a biocapacitator,
    "For what it's worth, let them build biocapacitators,"
she said to her dad on the phone,
she was not at all content with the fact that they'd build a biocapacitator
right under her feet,
and with having to find a new place to put her bike
and with having to remove her stuff from the locker.

The government announcement had been
that the building of biocapacitators

was in the interest of
all Canadians
and that
all Canadians
benefit from biocapacitators,
and that the federal government was to make sure that the interest of
all Canadians
was protected against the so-called 'special interests' of
actual, individual Canadians,
like the egoistical desire to live without a biocapacitator
   in the basement.

At first, Brenda wanted to just disobey
which conveniently would have meant to do nothing.
She also wanted to talk to her neighbours, having vague ideas about
   a common resistance
which, however, did not materialize
primarily because she shied away from knocking at their doors,
and instead sat on her couch, disobediently watching YouTube videos.

But in the evening before the government deadline, Brenda got nervous
and eventually moved most of her stuff out of the locker.
She left *some* stuff inside, to test how far they would go,
but made sure it was not really important stuff
like two broken lamps,
some comedy records from the '50s which her fifth boyfriend had left
   when they split up
and
a plastic bag
full of plastic bags.
She thought
the government would have to deal with that:
   "If they want their biocapacitator, they can remove that junk
     themselves,"
she said to her mom on the phone.

When she came home from work the next day
and had a quick look into the basement,

she found all the storage lockers empty
and lots of red hazard tape,
warning that unauthorized people had no access
   to this part of the building anymore.
She also found a letter in her mailbox
informing her that some of her items had been taken away
but could still be picked up at a certain government office downtown.

She also found a handwritten note at her door
which called for an emergency meeting of all tenants
that very evening.

At the meeting
at first, some people stressed that since the building was on
unceded territory
of…
some…
First Nation whose exact name they could not remember right now,
any government action was illegal anyway
without prior informed consent of the involved First Nation…
bands… or…
whatever
— and all the white people agreed.

Then somebody said that in Quebec, the building of biocapacitators
   had been halted
by initiatives, and it was suggested that somebody read up on that
on the internet.
Which was difficult because no one in the room spoke French,
but Brenda and a woman from the third floor spoke some Spanish,
so they volunteered for that.

It needs to be said that
the whole meeting proceeded in a certain mood of unease
which to some extent was caused by the fact that
no one in the room actually knew what a biocapacitator is
and a bearded guy from the second floor consistently
called them 'biocompressors' instead

whereafter several people got unsure and referred to them as
'these things'
or 'B.C.s'
and made general statements about
the bad impact of B.C.s on the environment
and the feeling that B.C.s did not bring as many jobs
    as the B.C. industry alleged.

Brenda left the meeting with mixed feelings
among them
the cursing of her initials
which she now had to share not only with that province she lived in,
but also with some technical device
whose exact functionality, purpose and even name were unclear to her.
But also
with the feeling that at least she had gotten to know
    some of her neighbours better
like the woman from the third floor who had co-volunteered to read up
    on the Québécois stuff
which they sort of did, but over the next weeks they also
just met for coffees and chat
and realized they both liked the same cake place downtown
which happened to be right next to the government office
    where the junk was.
    "Let's meet there tomorrow. I'll pick up my stuff beforehand,"
Brenda said to her new friend on the phone,
and they actually met there the next day
and Brenda told her neighbour that she
had retrieved her ex's comedy records
but defiantly had denied possession of the broken lamps
and finally, had not been keen enough to ask for
her plastic bag full of plastic bags
which for some unspecified reason
was of a certain nostalgic value to her.

Brenda Craigdarroch's Famous Raisin Cookies

Every time Brenda Craigdarroch made her famous raisin cookies,
she had to think about how crappy the new *X-Files* episodes had been.
She could not help it.
The first time, that thought just randomly passed through her mind
at the moment when she poured the raisins into the batter.
As it sometimes happens, you suddenly think of something
for a few seconds
without apparent reason.
You might be writing a birthday card to your cousin
and suddenly think of an old Coca-Cola commercial;
or be preparing a college lecture on Russian novelists
and suddenly remember a ping-pong game you lost
   on a school excursion;
or be walking around a lake
and suddenly think of Pierre, not Justin, Trudeau.
So that just happened — Brenda poured the raisins into the batter
which she had prepared in the medium-sized red bowl,
and at that moment
she suddenly thought of the new *X-Files* episodes,
and the next moment she thought
what complete and utter shit those new episodes had been,
and then she lost that thought and thought about something else.
Maybe... lightbulbs.

But,
the next time she made her famous raisin cookies,

41

two months later or so,
at the very moment she poured the raisins into the batter
which she had prepared in the medium-sized red plastic bowl,
an image shot to her mind
of Mulder and Scully in a cabin in the woods
and there she thought again
how
with the possible exception of half an episode,
they all were outrageously crazy horseshit,
really horribly bad, uninteresting,
pathetically poorly written and filmed
and, for long awkward sequences, just dumb as fuck.
And
Brenda remembered
that she had had
that exact same thought
the last time she had made her famous raisin cookies.
True, soon again she thought of something else
and when she put the tray into the oven,
there was nothing *X-Files*-related on her mind anymore,
but after this it was a lost cause.

Even though she completely forgot about it
for the next couple of weeks,
even when she had a conversation
with her brother-in-law
which touched upon the *X-Files* for a few back-and-forths,
wherein she certainly enforced her view about the new episodes,
she did not think of the raisin cookie incident
until eventually
Brenda made her famous raisin cookies again.
She got the medium-sized red bowl out
(which she had used for a dozen other things in the meantime),
she made the batter
(still clear of thoughts of anything related to mystery TV shows),
put the raisins in and *BOOM!*
How unbelievably disappointing were those new *X-Files* episodes:
miserable,

dreadful,
cockamamie.

That
went through her mind and, at the same time,
she distinctly remembered that she had already had that thought
    the last two times she had made her raisin cookies,
and then she knew that from now on she would be cursed;
apparently by now, her brain had
wired
her annoyance at the new *X-Files* episodes
to the moment when she poured raisins into the cookie batter in the
    medium-sized red plastic bowl;
she knew this would happen again and again
for *of course* she would occasionally make her famous raisin cookies
and *of course* she would always use that red plastic bowl for that
without thinking of any mystery series from the '90s
neither the *X-Files*
    nor *Dark Skies*
    nor *Quantum Leap*
    nor *The Visitor*
    nor *Seven Days*
    nor *Time Trax*
    nor *Millennium*
    nor the '90s remakes of the *Twilight Zone* and *The Outer Limits*
she would not have her mind on that
    but when the moment came to pour the raisins into the batter
the *X-Files* would come up again,
and her disappointment,
mixed with a minor confusion about the crush she used to have
    on David Duchovny,
or rather on the character he played, back in the '90s,
a crush which never even sparked again during the new episodes;
she had been mildly excited to see whether she would
    still have that crush,
but when she watched the new episodes, she felt
nothing for his character,
or any of the characters,

nothing
but embarrassment.

This embarrassment
and her whole *X-Files* complex
and on top of it, the thought that it was now trigger-wired
to a specific step in the preparation of raisin cookies,
this time
stayed on her mind for a bit longer,
    all through the shaping of the cookies
and up until putting them into the oven, only then fading away
or rather being replaced by an erotic fantasy about a coworker
    and a question about seagulls.

She went through the breakup with her sixth boyfriend at that time
and made no raisin cookies for many months.

When she made them again, finally, for her classmates
in a course on the influence of Russian novelists
    on David Foster Wallace,
the moment she poured the raisins into the batter,
BOOM! Fox Mulder was not sexy anymore.
Not even interesting in a platonic way.
And that, even though this time
she had used
the big red bowl,
not the medium-sized one,
because she had wanted to make enough cookies for all the people
in her Russian novelists and David Foster Wallace class.

So, accepting her curse, she just thought on
about the crapness
of the new *X-Files* episodes
and how she never wanted to watch the old *X-Files* episodes again
for fear that they would seem just as silly to her now as the new ones
and her mind walked her through
the general disappointment she felt about many so-called
remakes and relaunches and franchise extensions and homages,

and with a resigned exasperation pondered
while her hands formed sad raisin cookies:
    why do these people do that?
    why do they keep making sequels and remakes and extensions
        and homages
    inevitably failing and spoiling the original?
    even with good sequels, you can just spoil the original.
Brenda thought
while forming more cookies for her Russian novelists class
    how
    Gogol had destroyed the sequel he had written
        to his novel *Dead Souls*
    and rightly so, the parts which were saved *are* bad,
    the scholars, in their commentaries, try to hide behind
        scholarly words,
    you can feel their embarrassment, they write that
        what survived of the second part is
    "not quite at the level of the first part" or
    "he seems to have struggled with this" or
    "these chapters still need some redaction"
    which is all horseshit and cowardly words for
    this is crap,
    apparently Gogol had lost it; let's be happy with the first part
    and forget about this new shit.
    Gogol actually went insane
    probably because he knew that whatever he tried to write
        after *Dead Souls*
    would just appear as crap,
    so he burned it and went insane,
        or,
Brenda thought on
as the oven was preheating
    Dostoevsky, he wrote *The Brothers Karamazov*
    and called it the first part,
    but kept it quite self-contained
    and then
    Dostoevsky,
    instead of writing the second part,

just died.
He just died, of old age,
not even of one of those fancy Russian-novelist-deaths
like epilepsy, or bankruptcy, or tuberculosis, or suicide,
he just died of old age, thereby abstaining from writing,
and spoiling,
a sequel to *The Brothers Karamazov*.

So, Brenda thought
when she angrily shut the oven door
    why could those people in Hollywood
    not burn their film after making sequels
    or format their hard drives
    or just die?
    but that
Brenda thought while she angrily set the timer
    would not help.
    Now, they boost stuff with recently deceased people in it.

This is the sentence Brenda thought when she put on the timer:
    Death could stop Gogol and Dostoevsky from ruining sequels
    and writing shitty new *X-Files* episodes,
    but in our time, not even death can stop people
    from making sequels and remakes or parodies and homages,
    in fact, death seems to spur them,
    once an artist dies other people seem to think that now is the time to
    'honour'
    them with homages and adapting their style
    as it happened to Nabokov
    and it happened to Bukowski
    and it happened to Bernhard
    and it happened to David Foster Wallace
but, Brenda thought,
gesturing on her dining chair where she was now waiting
    for the cookies to bake
    David Foster Wallace fucking killed himself
    and that is in the back of your head if you want it or not
    when you read his stuff, of course you can and should

look at most of it
for a long time
without thinking that David Foster Wallace fucking killed himself
but it would be wrong to ignore that fact completely —
if you want to make a complete and detailed and
  differentiated assessment of the situation
you will have to regard the fact that David Foster Wallace
  fucking killed himself
and of course you will have to say that, basically,
  what the fuck do you know
   and who the fuck are you to assess that and all these things are
   as complicated as life and death
   and what do we know about the interrelation of the
   life and death of a writer on the one hand
   and their writing on the other?
well, you can assess David Foster Wallace's writing
  with all the methods of
  literature theory and art theory and whatever theory
  and you might even invent some new theory,
and on the other hand you can state the fact that
  David Foster Wallace fucking killed himself,
but what method do you have
  and what clue do you have
  and what right do you have
  to somehow speculate about connections of one to the other?
well, you can say you *have* every right
but then what do you say? do you say that he filled his books
  with obsessive footnotes
and just trust that the word 'obsessive' will sound
  as if there's a hint, there's a trace?
but if you look closer, do you want to say that
  he just wrote too many
  obsessive footnotes
and that David Foster Wallace fucking killed himself
  because he wrote
  too many obsessive footnotes?
was it the obsessive footnotes that pushed David Foster Wallace
  over the edge,

would he *not* have fucking killed himself if he had written fewer
  obsessive footnotes,
and what, fifty obsessive footnotes less,
or twenty, or ten, or five, was it three specific obsessive footnotes that
  he should *not*
  have written, would that have made all the difference?
but then you say, you know what,
maybe he did not write enough obsessive footnotes,
maybe he wrote one obsessive footnote too few,
maybe one more obsessive footnote would have saved him,
or ten more, or fifty more,
maybe he was a hundred obsessive footnotes short of being an
  obsessive writer who does *not* fucking kill himself,
maybe in a hundred obsessive footnotes more he would have found
  something that would have made him not fucking kill himself
  or just kept him interested or busy or
  occupied with something that would have
  distracted him from fucking killing himself
maybe just for ten minutes and then somebody
  would have called him
and he would not have fucking killed himself at least on that day
and maybe not for the next week or some months or even years,
who knows?
Well, I don't, you don't, nobody does, that is the fucking problem,
nobody has a clue and the fact remains that David Foster Wallace
  fucking killed himself,
and all talking about whether this was
  somehow related to his writing and his writing style
  and whether he wrote one obsessive footnote too much or
  too few is just empty talk
and probably the obsessive footnotes have fuck-nothing to do
  with the fact
that David Foster Wallace fucking killed himself
but the fact remains
that David Foster Wallace fucking killed himself.

Brenda thought when the timer rang for the first ten minutes
  And also, nobody should try to imitate his style,

48

regardless of whether he fucking killed himself or not
— that is on a different planet —
no one should try to imitate anybody else's style,
Brenda thought when she checked the cookies,
regardless of whether that someone has fucking killed himself
or burnt his manuscripts or just died
of tuberculosis, bankruptcy or old age,
and especially no one should try to imitate someone else's style
as an homage or parody.
homages and parodies are the two dumbest forms of expression
and also the dumbest forms of admiration,
Brenda thought while she set the timer for five more minutes
and the raisin cookie scent filled the air
see, Dostoevsky admired Pushkin,
but he would neither try to imitate nor parody Pushkin,
knowing full well that the truest spirit of admiration for an artist is
to just leave the admired art alone and create your own work
and if Gogol came back today
and Tolstoy came back today
and Dostoevsky came back today
they might admire their own old writings
but they would not write in that style today,
but in a new one, a very distinct one,
something distinct even from Nabokov,
and if David Foster Wallace would not have fucking killed himself,
well, okay,
he might still write in his obsessive footnote style,
but if instead he remained fucking dead and would be reborn
fifty years from now
he would quite certainly just shit on
the old David Foster Wallace style
and not write obsessive footnotes anymore,
not even as homage or parody,
and maybe he would not write literature at all,
he would just shoot at old doors with paintballs
or bake raisin cookies
or conspire with the reborn Russian novelists
to burn down film studios

and the mansions of TV executives
and kidnap the mothers of every homage-writing screenwriter
and create live art performances
where they all together literally shit on hard-copy scripts of
every relaunch of every mildly successful TV show
and every sequel to every movie that tries to
"stay true" and "pay homage" to the original and
"develops the story in a sensible and interesting direction"
which is all fucking horseshit and the
cowardly way for film reviewers to say
that it did not need to be made,
hence should not have been made
and Gogol would have burned it
    and Dostoevsky would simply have died.

This is the sentence that Brenda thought
when the timer rang and her famous raisin cookies were hot and ready:
    Gogol would have burned it
    and Dostoevsky would simply have died.

Brenda Craigdarroch
and Her Dentist

Brenda Craigdarroch's girlfriends never figured out
exactly when, where and how Brenda had developed the notion
that her dentist had a crush on her.

Andrea, who'd known Brenda for the longest time,
remembered vividly that
Brenda had uttered something to that effect
during a long car ride the two of them had taken
from Kamloops to Calgary,
as well as the lighthearted conversation which followed
and had them laughing lots
whilst driving through the Rocky Mountains.
That car ride, however,
took place not very long ago,
in the summer when Brenda and Andrea had reconnected
after running into each other in a Zumba class.
Andrea had known Brenda previously in high school
but they had been out of touch for some years after that.
In Andrea's view, it was unlikely
but not impossible
that Brenda had already conceived of her dentist having a crush on her
    when she was in high school,
and just had not shared that with Andrea
who had not been particularly close to Brenda back then.
Also, as far as Andrea remembered,
in their high school time,

51

Brenda had not been a person who would share
  lots of private details with anyone anyway.

Cassidy, who had taken Brenda in as her roomie for two months
after Brenda's breakup with her fourth boyfriend,
learned about the issue when, one day,
she was surprised to see Brenda dress up a bit,
and Cassidy teased her for not telling her about her date,
to which Brenda replied that she *wasn't* going on a date,
just going out to a dentist appointment
and to buy some groceries,
and some body lotion,
and an impact wrench at her favourite hardware store.
Cassidy did not let her off the hook
and although one can find some justification
  for dressing a bit nicer than usual
when running errands as those,
it was impossible even for Brenda to get a sound argument working
for putting on lipstick before seeing her dentist,
especially since Brenda was not a person who would normally wear
  lipstick anyway.
So eventually Brenda confessed
but stressed that of course she did not reciprocate
the feelings her dentist supposedly had for her
and that she was just in a bit of a mess because of her recent breakup.

Isbel, Brenda's most consistent friend over the years,
who'd forgotten when she'd first heard of Brenda's dentist's
  purported philandering
    — it was just something that Brenda mentioned as an aside
  in half-sentences
  at odd times, maybe twice a year
  during chat over lunch —
Isbel was the one who *almost* brought it up to the other girlfriends
one night when they were all out for tapas
but Brenda was home due to a bad cold.
And if Isbel *had* brought it up
and said,

"Hey, I guess you've heard that story from Brenda too
    that,
    you know,
    she thinks
    her dentist
    sort of
    secretly
    flirts with her,"
then they would all have said
    "Oh yes!"
     and
    "Yeah, that's a bit weird, right?"
and putting together the bits of information each of them
    had on the topic
they would soon have gathered
that Brenda had been insisting on her dentist's courting
    and subtle advances
for more than fourteen years,
and further
that Brenda had had at least four different dentists in that time,
    three male, one female,
and all things considered,
the girlfriends would then have passed a motion
that one of them,
probably Zoltana,
should, on the next occasion, break the news to Brenda
that her girlfriends
with all the love and respect that they had for her
and knowing full well that Brenda was not a person who has *idées fixes*
or delusional preoccupations
— normally —
would have to tell her that her dentist's
gentleness, special care and affection for her and only her
most probably existed only in her head
and that the dentist's
winks, gestures and bum shakes
if they existed at all
were almost certainly misinterpreted by her.

But
Isbel never brought it up
and they never put their pieces of the puzzle together
and no conversation containing the term 'delusional preoccupation'
    ever ensued,
probably for the better.

Zoltana
who by all accounts was "the weird one" among Brenda's girlfriends,
herself holding several beliefs with little connection to the
    commonly shared reality,
had heard Brenda mention her dentist's trifling only once
and had smiled about it, immediately assuming that
Brenda was aware of having made it up
as a coping mechanism, keeping it in a state of quarter-belief.
She thought it's probably nifty to have something vaguely uplifting
    to think about
when you are tied to a chair
with several expensive devices operating in your mouth,
and you have to make a hand gesture to ask for permission to swallow,
one of the most undignified positions a first-world person can get
    themselves into.
And Zoltana actually tried to tell herself the same thing
    at *her* next dentist appointment
looking for delicate signs of tenderness in her dentist's demeanour
and it worked for a while but utterly imploded
at the moment when her dentist,
    with that subtle-accusation-dentist-voice, said
    "Hmm, your gums are bleeding…?"
to which Zoltana replied
    "Yeah, because you just stabbed them with that metal hook!
    I guess if I rammed that thing into your eyeball, we'd see some
    bloodshed there as well."
But she did not actually say that;
instead, she lied about her flossing habits
and made the consciously false promise to intensify them
like any normal kind of person would.

Brenda Craigdarroch
and the Last Piece of Art

The last piece of art which Brenda Craigdarroch remembered
as having a lasting and profound impact on her
was
the last five pages of a story
in a pulp magazine she had read
when she was very, very bored
at a friend's friend's open house party.

That is what she said
when her fifth boyfriend once asked her
what works of art had made
a profound and lasting impact on her.
And she was serious,
because that story,
or the last five pages of the story,
in which somehow
a rotten oak leaf
played an important role,
truly had stuck in her memory.

But she was happy that this answer was also
a gentle rebuff to his question.
Brenda liked art,
but she did not like to talk about art,
mostly because she really did not know what to say.
Especially if the work of art was good:

She would just say
   "That's good"
but find herself unable to elaborate on that,
just as she felt unable to contribute
when people talked about art
or about music
or about books.
Brenda, rather, talked about her life
   and her job
   and people
   and food
   and memories
   and beaches
   and prophecies
   and the right time to prune lilac.

But when people talked about what a certain arthouse film
   meant to them
or how a certain famous painting shows
that the artist overcame an early period of their work,
Brenda got annoyed
and tried to steer the conversation away from that
and towards masturbation techniques.

She found that instead of talking about a sculpture
and which sculpting style it belongs to,
people would be much happier if they shared
little hidden sorrows, and talked about
things all of us secretly have, but are afraid to talk about:
Like silverfish
or the occasional feeling of being an impostor.

And instead of talking about a symphony or violin concerto
or an exhibition inspired by a symphony or violin concerto
or a videogame inspired by an exhibition about a symphony
   or violin concerto,
people should rather open up a bit amongst their friends
and talk about the things all of us want to have:

Like good sex
and opinions.

The worst kind of talk about art, in Brenda's eyes,
were the little explanatory cards next to paintings
   in art galleries and museums
on which somebody who needs to show off that they went to school
talks about an artist and their art,
but which never
had the least thing to do with any sensation Brenda had
   when *she* looked at the paintings.
They were not even wrong, they just seemed to talk
about something that was *way off.*
They might as well have contained descriptions of the geysers on Triton
or instructions to use a VCR —
in any case, something extremely alien to what Brenda thought and felt
when she was walking through a gallery and looking at paintings.
Actually, Brenda rarely thought anything that could be
   expressed in sentences
whilst walking through a gallery and looking at paintings.
She liked many of the paintings,
she appreciated a lot of the art,
some of it even had a profound and lasting impact on her,
but did not set her mind to dancing;
rather,
every time Brenda walked through an art gallery
   and looked at paintings
it made her want to sing.
And every time Brenda was in a concert,
   she felt like she wanted to sculpt,
and every time Brenda saw sculptures,
   she wanted to knit something or work with felt,
and every time Brenda saw craft,
   she wanted to own a huge park and spend every day there,
landscaping:
putting in rocks
planning streams
planting trees

(Asian, Alpine, olive trees, ginkgos)
a greenhouse full of lemons
meadows with wildflowers
etc. —
that's what Brenda fantasized about when she was at a craft fair.
But whenever Brenda walked in an actual park,
  she just wanted to mix cocktails.

She had mixed a good Basil Smash
for her boyfriend and herself that night when,
after watching a documentary about gannets and boobies,
somehow their conversation had moved on to art
and he had asked her what works of art had had
a lasting and profound impact on her.
Brenda had said those five pages from the pulp magazine
of which she mostly remembered something about a rotten oak leaf,
and her boyfriend began talking about some comedy records
  from the '50s
which had had a lasting and profound impact on him
until he realized he should just keep her company silently.
Brenda, in her head, remembered that story from the pulp magazine
or its last pages
wherein the main character and her partner
set out for an expedition in some kind of fog
which lifted after a while, when they heard the sound of water
and found a stream which they then followed for many kilometres,
first across rocky terrain
then between trees
eventually encountering houses, then paved roads,
sidewalks interspersed with oak trees,
then the outskirts of some city,
and the story got a bit weird from there
and the main thing which Brenda remembered was
that there was something about a rotten oak leaf
which the two characters had seen on the pavement —
the rest was blurry and she was not sure if it had been part of that story,
  or of another story,
or some film she had seen…

well, there was a part where the two of them were fighting an army
    of 580 androids
who all looked like Doug Ford
and there was more changing of the weather:
the fog got thicker and thinner again.
But through all of that, the one thing of importance
was that rotten oak leaf,
and maybe something about the way it lay there in the dirt
and how the light fell on it
or how it smelled
— that brown, rotten oak leaf —
somehow the writer had given meaning to that rotten oak leaf
between all the other things that were going on in those five pages,
some climactic action occurred,
something about the relation between the friends was revealed,
but through it all,
the one thing that Brenda remembered
clearly, but vaguely, but clearly,
was that rotten oak leaf.

Brenda Craigdarroch
and the Dead Robin in the Gutter

The day Brenda Craigdarroch saw a dead robin in the gutter
and, beside it, a half-eaten pear
was one of the most eventful days Brenda had had in a while.

The morning of that day was not that eventful,
— it was quite ordinary actually —
with some computer issues at the office job she was working then,
but filled with unusual excitement because Brenda was going
    to meet her sister
for the first time since the previous April.
Her sister had told her the day before that she would be in town
and they had agreed to meet during Brenda's lunch break
at a Kalmykian restaurant.

It was on the walk over to the Kalmykian restaurant
that Brenda saw the dead robin in the gutter
and, beside it, the half-eaten pear.
Two blocks further
she met her sister in front of the restaurant.
They hugged each other, more cordially than the last few times,
and had a nice lunch
at the Kalmykian restaurant.
Her sister told Brenda that her husband had switched jobs
which was quite a surprise,
and showed Brenda pictures of their dog
which were quite cute.

Brenda showed her sister the new rain jacket she had bought
(her sister liked it),
and pictures of the weekend trip to Cowichan Lake
where she had gone with her neighbour-friend
and at some point Brenda mentioned
the dead robin in the gutter
and, beside it, the half-eaten pear
which she had seen on her walk over,
and her sister said
   "That's a still life!"

Later, during dessert, Brenda and her sister played a game they had
   started when they were teenagers,
where each of them had to come up with something they would do if
   they were incredibly rich.
When they were teenagers, they had come up with things like:
ordering a 50-inch TV set,
ordering an axe,
smashing the TV set with the axe,
putting the debris in a box, sending it back to the retailer,
complaining about a malfunction
and asking for a refund
to see how they would react.

They were more grown-up now.
So Brenda said she would buy a golf course —
then, have eighteen slides
in eighteen different colours
put on the greens,
have vines planted besides the slides,
further, hire eighteen security guards
who all had to be friendly single moms
whose only job it was to make sure the vines were not being damaged,
so the slides would be free to use for anyone
until one day the vines had overgrown them.

Brenda's sister said she would drive her car into a shopping mall
leaving it up for grabs in the smashed glass front,

then buy some minor items from the shops,
before just buying the entire mall
and turning the ground level into a play area,
the second level into a research centre
of which three-quarters would investigate cancer
but one quarter was set aside to investigate
    the most efficient way to grow
shaggy cap mushrooms on the rooftop of a former mall building.
And the rooftop, she would turn into
    a shaggy cap mushroom plantation.

They agreed that Brenda's sister had won this one
for the cancer research and for the detail of
first buying minor items before taking over the mall,
but Brenda got extra points for a project
    which showed its beauty in the long run
and for paying single mothers.
And then they concluded, as always,
    by fretting about *actual* rich people
who die of drugs, boredom, loneliness,
and the inescapable void in their souls.

Next, right after saying goodbye to her sister
(more cordially than the last time),
Brenda got a text message that her employer's IT department
had had to shut down their entire system
and she would be off work for the afternoon.
And just as she was reading that
on the walk back from the Kalmykian restaurant,
she bumped into Cassidy,
her roommate from six years ago.
She told her what had just happened and that she was free all afternoon,
and Cassidy said she was also free for the next half-hour,
so they went into the next coffee shop and chatted.

Cassidy was the only person Brenda knew
besides herself
who would blow-dry her toes.

Brenda had seen that once when Cassidy had left
    the bathroom door ajar
and when they laughed and talked about it
they both felt the strange sensation that you feel
when you have a certain habit
about which you're not sure how common it is
and you never bring it up because
it's halfway between potentially embarrassing and too unimportant,
plus, it does not connect well to anything
    you would normally have a conversation about
but now, naturally by accident,
    you notice someone else has the same habit.

So they actually talked about that over coffee now.
They also wondered what is the correct past tense of 'blow-dry'.
And Cassidy mentioned her new purse.
And Brenda mentioned the dead robin she had seen in the gutter
and, beside it, the half-eaten pear.
And Cassidy said
    "That's so sad!"
And Brenda disagreed
but did not say that.

At that moment, there was a sudden noise,
so loud that several people went outside to inquire;
apparently, at a construction site at the other end of the block
there had been an explosion, with metal parts flying around,
but by a very lucky coincidence, nobody had been injured.

When the situation had calmed down, Cassidy said she had to go now,
    but mentioned
that their old mutual friend Marc was hosting an open house party
    tonight
and that she could not attend, but maybe Brenda wanted to go.
And Brenda said
    "Yeah, why not?"
And Cassidy replied
    "Yeah, why not?"

(The "Why not?" had been a thing between Brenda and Cassidy when
   they were roomies.)

So after Cassidy had to leave,
Brenda remembered Marc, the host of the party:
When Brenda had first met him
six years ago
he told her that he would soon go to Tibet
to find enlightenment;
he would just have to finish a few important projects first.
And Brenda had found that quite fascinating
and spent some time with him
and tried to connect with him
but it somehow did not really work out
and also, Brenda had fallen in love with her fifth boyfriend at that time.

Getting back to the present, Brenda called her then-boyfriend
(the sixth one) and negotiated about going to that party later.
He was a bit reluctant
but finally agreed that they would go
under the premise that he was allowed to drink and she would drive.
Brenda agreed
and told him about the dead robin in the gutter
and, beside it, the half-eaten pear
and he said
   "That's a good symbol.
   I just don't know what for."

At the party
Brenda chatted with Marc the host for a while
who seemed just as nice and smart as she remembered him
and she thought that she wanted to connect with him
and wondered why she had not done so years ago.

Later, Brenda ended up talking mostly to a slender old man
   with long hair
who could not even convincingly explain to her
   what he was doing at the party

65

and how he was connected to Marc the host
because every time he tried, he got into telling a story
    that went off on a tangent
    and then a tangent's tangent
and ended up talking about something else
which was or was not interesting in its own right
but could not satisfactorily explain his very presence
and at some point he looked Brenda in the eyes and said
that the hardest thing he had to face in life
was seeing the traces of his younger life disappear.
Brenda didn't know what to say to that
so she instead told him that today she had seen
a dead robin in the gutter
and, beside it, a half-eaten pear
and the old man said
    "Hm."

Then, after getting a last non-alcoholic drink,
Brenda located her boyfriend in the crowd
who seemed to need her help to get away from a guy
that had insisted that the moon landing was a hoax
and linked that to other conspiracy theories
whereupon Brenda's boyfriend insisted that recently,
    the guy who fixes his e-bike
shared a story with him, in person and via email,
about that e-bike dealer's cousin, who is an astronaut,
and how a few months ago, in real life, she'd been launched to the
    International Space Station
and some of her family members,
    including her cousin, the e-bike dealer,
had been invited to travel
to the actual Russian rocket launch station
near the actual Kazakh city of Baikonur
where they could actually see
the actual astronaut cousin of the e-bike dealer walking to her rocket
and that rocket being shot into space.
Brenda's boyfriend was now getting out his phone
to find that email from his e-bike dealer

with the pictures of his e-bike dealer's astronaut cousin
and to open a site where you could track the ISS
on which she, the actual astronaut cousin of his actual e-bike dealer, was
   at this very moment,
and Brenda's boyfriend was just coming to his big argument
and was about to bluntly ask the conspiracy theorist
   whether he believes
that all these people in all the space programs
   in the US and Russia and worldwide
and the engineers and physicists and proud parents in these pictures
and the mathematicians who compute the flight curves
and his e-bike dealer and his e-bike dealer's astronaut cousin
were all part of a big conspiracy and cover-up for the moon landing
   having been filmed in some film studio in Hollywood,
but at that point,
Marc the host of the party started a big speech
about his life and his friends and how grateful he was
and how sorry that some day soon
he would have to leave them all
because he would go to Tibet
and find enlightenment,
some time soon,
after finishing just a few more projects he was working on right now.
Brenda pulled her boyfriend away
and into the car
where on the way home, he continued to agitate
   against conspiracy theories
calling them
   "a contagious form of mind cancer
   which is spreading in our society"
and Brenda just nodded until he finally calmed down
and thanked her for getting him out,
saying he'd have to work early tomorrow
and asked Brenda how her day was,
and she told him that it had been quite eventful.

And later, after he had gone to bed, Brenda took out her diary,
whereinto she had not written anything in four months,

and although in her head she did a quick recap of
all the events, meetings and conversations, and explosions,
which had happened that day,
the one thing Brenda wrote down in her diary
was that today, she had seen
a dead robin in the gutter
and, beside it, a half-eaten pear.

Brenda Craigdarroch
Tried Hard To Forget Things

Brenda Craigdarroch tried hard to forget things.
For sure, she occasionally tried hard to remember something,
but she also tried to develop the skill of
focussing on one thing to forget, like
the PIN to her old bank card which she kept mixing up
   with the new one
or that time she had blanked on an exam
   which made her unnecessarily nervous it could happen again
or her mother's one-time rant about Brenda's grandfather,
on one of the long drives home from his house years ago,
which had been born of unfair momentary rage,
   as her mother herself conceded later.

To forget specific things like those
was a subtle undertaking, because naturally if someone
who is not skilled in the art of forgetting
focusses on something
they just end up engraving it deeper into their memory.
Instead, you have to somehow
deliberately *not* focus on something
but not by coincidental distraction or ignorance, rather
permanently, sort of
mindfully not paying attention,
smoothly making it smaller,
making it
go away,

which was a very delicate process
with many setbacks.

Brenda sometimes found that unfair, considering how easily
she could forget, say, where the hell she put the mug
which she'd taken out of the cupboard twenty seconds ago.

She wanted to forget her first boyfriend entirely,
she wanted to forget some bad things about her third boyfriend
    because they were bad,
and she wanted to forget some good things about her fifth boyfriend
    because remembering those good things made her miss him.

By the very nature of forgetting
Brenda did not know exactly what she had successfully forgotten;
she was certain it was a lot
because, when she tried to remember events or people
a lot seemed to be missing;
for example,
she remembered
the last time she had seen her grandfather,
last August,
but looking at, say, the second half of last September,
she was quite sure that she'd gone to work during weekdays,
but beyond that, there was just a blank.
There were holes in her memory
sometimes with a vague feeling
that there had been something
but it was no longer there.
Sometimes she tried to forget even these blurry holes
and was happy when
her mind achieved
just a blank stare
on the bus
where instead of revisiting tatters of memory,
she saw some of the houses along the road for the first time,
or the trees.
Later, she wondered if this was really the first time she'd seen them

or if she had seen them many times before
and then deliberately forgotten them
to get back the sensation of seeing them for the first time.

Although that was impossible for some of the houses
Brenda thought
because they looked newly-built,
so at best she had managed to forget the construction site
    that had been there before
or maybe trees which had been there before that.
But why would she have forgotten those?
She tried to not forget trees, only man-made buildings,
edifices and equipments,
only fleeting things that come and go.
Which is weird
Brenda thought
because wouldn't you remember the fleeting things that come and go,
as opposed to things that stay around anyway?
Memory is only good for the fleeting things that come and go
Brenda thought
but the trees are of a third kind, she thought:
they only go
now,
they never come
have always been there
even if in some distant past they maybe were not there yet
but they *have* been there as long as we have been there
    seem permanent
    continuous, immutable
    steady
    constant
    there every time you sit on the bus
until one day
you sit on the bus and they are no longer there.
Like her grandfather.

Brenda remembered
her grandfather used to say

that the problem with most people is
that they have nothing they *really wanna do.*
He said,
if you have something you *really wanna do,*
then you get rid of all the things you have to do
so that you can do what you *really wanna do;*
but if you have *nothing* you really wanna do,
then you just stare at all the things you *have* to do
and never finish them or, if you finish them,
you look for more things you have to do
and spend a lot of time talking about what you *have* to do
and you do this and that
and buy this and that which pretends to save time
  but you know damn well it doesn't
like fancy coffee machines or automatic garage doors
they pretend to make life easier,
  but you know damn well you will end up with
more you *have* to do.
But if there is something you *really wanna do,*
you will just quickly
and without much talk
get over all things that are in the way
so that you are free for
that one thing
you really wanna do.

For Brenda's grandfather, that thing was gardening.
And he was always willing to do other things if they *needed* to be done,
but then he would get them done
simply
silently
so that he would be able to work in his garden again.

But he said it can be anything,
the thing you really want to do.
It can be cooking.
It can be skating.
It can be painting.

It can be playing chess.
It can be chasing pigeons in the park.
It can be making up new constellations in the night sky.
For him, it was gardening.

That, Brenda did not want to forget.
Nor the long drives home from her grandparents' in the dark
with her mother driving
and herself, a girl in the backseat,
breathing against the car window
looking over her condensed breath
out into the night sky
and seeing the same constellations
that they had made up in her grandparents' garden
unchanged behind the trees and poles flashing by.
And the same moon,
weirdly, still in the same direction.
And herself just looking out
and drawing little figures and smiley faces on the steamed car window.

Brenda Craigdarroch's
Correct Opinions

One day in her late 20s, Brenda Craigdarroch realized
that she was
the only person
who on all matters of real importance
had the exact right opinion.

There were many issues she did not care about
and many whereabout she admitted having insufficient insight.
It's not like she would get into a debate about
what food might improve one's weather resistance.
But
about the couple of things that she did care about
like climate change
or had studied with some passion
like the writings of Gogol
and the pros and cons of flossing
or had as hobbies, like do-it-yourself home improvement,
she was consistently right.
Of course she was, for why would she uphold a wrong belief
on a topic that she deeply cared about *and* had researched?!?
Notwithstanding vague views she might have on things
    of secondary importance
where she relied on a mix of high school knowledge, common sense and
    her filter bubble,
her views on a few issues dear to her heart
were well-informed and balanced,

carefully measuring evidence against counterevidence and altogether
forming a coherent network of mutually reinforcing viewpoints,
which, after all, were shared by most of her friends.
That is how Brenda *knew* she was right.
As for each of the issues,
practically everyone she knew had the same view.
Everyone agreed with her stance on abortion
(except her brother-in-law, who had been raised on a farm though).
Everyone agreed that advertisements should be banned
except that weird lady from the other office in her job in 2008
and Zoltana,
although with Zoltana you never knew if she was being ironic.
Everyone agreed that the death penalty is wrong
except her second boyfriend, but he was a jerk, she knew now,
and notwithstanding the sad state of the debate on capital punishment
wherein some people, like her neighbour-friend,
although they ultimately agreed with Brenda,
did so for the wrong reasons.

Be that as it may, for each viewpoint Brenda had,
the people who agreed with her were in the overwhelming majority,
she was part of a broad consensus of sensible people on all issues.

But
the truly striking part of that revelation Brenda had
one day in her late 20s
was not that *she* got things right on a variety of important topics;
she just had never thought that would make her special in any way.
She had expected that many people were like her, were with her,
that there would be a big chunk of people
who, like her, had the big questions fathomed,
notwithstanding that for a few isolated issues there would be
  a few isolated people who were a bit nuts.
What dawned on her now,
surprisingly and momentarily frightening,
was that there was no one who agreed with the correct view
(that happened to be Brenda's view)
on *all* issues.

Although on each single subject matter more than 90% were with her,
the intersection of those sets contained
only Brenda.
Even the most right-minded, sane, balanced people seemed to have
   one little quirk
where they disagreed with what almost everyone,
   including Brenda, thought.
For example, even her grandfather
who was one of the most rational people on Earth
had strange views as soon as physical health and medicine
   were involved;
one time he claimed that there's too many vaccinations these days,
and he never boarded an airplane, on the grounds that flying would kill
   thousands each year by thrombosis.

Or, her fourth and current boyfriend,
who could not stop mocking her for her vegetarianism.
Which was not a big deal,
   she mocked him back and they still got along,
but sometimes when Brenda was by herself, she found it a bit weird
that such a smart and knowledgeable person would,
on this one issue, hold a view which she could
tolerate
but which, ultimately, would be disproven by history
because it was wrong.
She thought, the only reasonable explanation is that
   he's not well-informed enough
and she could forgive him for that
although she felt he had sort of an obligation to educate himself better,
thereby coming to the right conclusion,
namely, to not eat meat, in a convinced but not preachy way,
doing this one little thing for oneself, because it's right,
notwithstanding that it was not automatically healthier, rather
seeing it as an opportunity to eat healthier anyway;
in short: to just settle on the exact same approach that Brenda had.

Brenda could not get over that, ever. She felt love for him anyway.
One night, he ate a hearty dinner,

while Brenda, on the couch, was trying to find at least
  one person in history
who, like her, had it basically figured out.
And when he had finished his mashed potatoes, onion rings,
  cabbage rolls and calf liver,
he asked her what she was thinking
and she replied,
    "How does this sound:
    Buddha, Muhammad, Jesus, Spinoza, Brenda Craigdarroch?"
And he replied
    "Know what? It's a non-sequitur but
    I'd really, really enjoy walking through a rain shower right now."

Brenda Craigdarroch's
Preferred Zodiac Sign

Whenever somebody wanted to create a horoscope
     for Brenda Craigdarroch
she would say that she *was* born in early September,
but did not identify as a Virgo;
her preferred zodiac sign was Capricorn.
She believed that in a society
that has come so far as to acknowledge
that your identity is not predetermined
     by the genitals you are born with,
equally little, or less,
is it predetermined by a random image
somebody decided to see in the stars that happen to be aligned with the
     sun on your birthday.
And she would not have anything about her personality
     inferred from those stars by anyone
who, Brenda suspected, would not be able to actually identify any of the
     zodiac constellations in the night sky,
nor accurately explain why the sun appears to move through them
     in the course of a year.

The truth is, though, that nobody ever asked Brenda Craigdarroch
     about her zodiac sign,
at least not since she had carefully drafted this reply a few years ago.
It was just a situation she imagined,
to prove something to herself,
like her sixth boyfriend for a time imagined

79

being invited to the White House
so that he could ostentatiously turn down that invitation.

When they were having cake at Brenda's favourite cake place
the one run by a German immigrant
    full of spite and great recipes,
    known as the cake nazi,
Brenda told her boyfriend that
his phantasies about turning down an invitation by Trump
or resigning from Trudeau's cabinet in solidarity
    with Philpott and Wilson-Raybould
were a typical sublimation of guilt by straight white men
which were not harmful in themselves, but not actually helpful either.
And in this way they became harmful,
because they gave those men the feeling of being right
without doing anything at all.
Her boyfriend admitted that seemed true
but added that
having the feeling of being right without actually doing anything
seemed to be the entire purpose of having opinions.
Brenda admitted that seemed true
and they concluded that having opinions should be regarded with
    much more skepticism than it usually is,
and that they should act against the overabundance of opinions
    in their daily lives.

Her boyfriend then,
whilst indulging in the last bits of his Frankfurter Kranz cake,
mentioned that a friend of his had been active on
    various internet forums
with two accounts, one with a male and one with a female username,
and reported that his female alter-ego
on engineering and programming forums
got a lot more upvotes and thumbs up and comments full of nice
    condescending praise,
on the other hand, she frequently received sexual harassment
    on a chess website
where his male version got insulted at most three times a year,

and then only with non-sexually charged insults
like "make a move, asshole" or "I'll block you, fucking cheating idiot."

Brenda,
taking a large sip of her coffee,
got a bit angry and said: well, good for your friend,
but he could have just listened to women who told him that
and believed *them* and report *that*.
But you have to hear it from a straight white man to believe it?
That's like those journalists who tried out waterboarding for themselves
as if that makes them and their audience understand
   what it's like to be tortured.

Her boyfriend said that saying "all straight white men do this"
was not better than saying "all Sagittarii do this,"
noting that twenty minutes ago Brenda had ranted that
   even if you could show
that Sagittarii statistically are more proactive
   or Librae are more balanced,
then that would be like saying that men are born fighters
   and women like ponies and the colour pink:
It's just that for centuries they have been brought up that way,
and maybe people have mentioned supposed character traits of
   Sagittarii just three times to a Sagittarius child
   which quickly internalized them;
just like there's no surer way to turn someone into a scoundrel than
   telling them they'll be a scoundrel
starting from an early age.

And wouldn't Brenda agree, her boyfriend continued,
just as the cake nazi had come to their table to take their dishes,
wouldn't she agree with his dream of a world where people would just
   be seen for their character and skills,
and not whether they identify as white or black or cis or trans
   or Leo or Gemini?

And before Brenda could retort with another well-crafted
   stock reply of hers

which stated that it's not so easy to imagine a clean canvas
when history has happened and injustice has already been done
and further
that the values of such an ostensibly colour-blind, gender-neutral utopia
oftentimes were surprisingly well-tailored to favour those who've
   internalized being straight white dudes,
and all in all she'd rather be a Capricorn,
a horned goat,
than a straight white dude,
the cake nazi
who was infamous for intruding on his patrons' conversations
said that
   "You young folks do realize zat
   you are now frree to be trruns
   and vear leggings
   or give yourself a spirichwal name
   but only as long as you still spend fifty hours a veek
   producing worsless shit nobody needs
   so viz ze money, you can vaste the rest of ze veek
   consuming worsless shit made by uzzers,
   do you?"

And Brenda said
   "Err... Can I have another piece of the chocolate cake?"
partly because the chocolate cake was really good
and partly because she did not want the cake nazi to have the last word.

Brenda Craigdarroch
and the Monolingual People

Brenda Craigdarroch could not help being biased
   against monolingual people
by which, in deviation from standard language,
she did not mean her fellow Canadians who
in an officially bilingual country somehow had managed to go through
   eight years of French in school
   and still barely understand
   the dual labels in the supermarket,
since Brenda was more or less one of them;
the only foreign language she spoke was vacational Spanish.

Also, it was not like she was fond
of those people she occasionally met,
especially in academic circles,
who apparently spoke three, four, five languages
and still had nothing interesting to say.

Her third boyfriend however
had known Java, C++, Python, R, html and, as a joke, BASIC,
and whenever asked about his language skills, casually remarked that he
   spoke nine,
namely the aforementioned
   plus English plus Punjabi plus math.

About that time, Brenda started to consider herself multilingual too,
whereby she meant the ability to understand

and make herself understood in
the languages of several cultures, milieus and peer groups.

From her upbringing, she was quite fluent in *liberal*;
in her 20s, she learned a decent *progressive* in an environmentalist
    dialect, although she never got the socialist accent right;
and on visits to her sister and brother-in-law
    she learned a few scraps of *conservative*.

Skills in all these languages were very handy
    especially at family gatherings,
at strata council meetings,
or when being introduced to a new boyfriend's parents.

She also had a good command of Hardware Store Jargon
and Sex Talk
and was eager to learn a few more languages
or try to get rid of the accent she still must have had
in Rural
or Family Gossiping
whose native speakers invariably looked askance at her
when she tried to fit in with a funny remark.

Sometimes late at night while sitting all by the internet
    with a glass of wine
she practised some of the old languages
and polished her Late Night Comedic
or Holistic Healthish,
two languages that were often spoken during coffee breaks at her job.

Regardless of the varying success of her own endeavours,
she was more and more annoyed by people
    who seemed to be willfully monolingual
although she did believe that greatness can only be achieved
    by focussing.
But in almost all cases she saw, monolinguals kept a *very* narrow focus
and *nothing* great ever came out of the fact that they
    would *only* and *at all times*

84

speak Christian
or News-ish
or that obnoxious jocular dialect of Business Talk.

Then there was the extreme case of her friend Rob from high school
who went on to study engineering
and whose only interest besides engineering was knitting.
Many former friends found that over the years
it became increasingly difficult to communicate with Rob the engineer,
and several eventually cut contact with him,
exasperated, annoyed,
saying he only talked rubbish now.
Brenda realized Rob did not talk rubbish:
he talked Robbish.
One mistook what he spoke for English and got irritated
because it was not English,
it just imitated the vocabulary and grammar of English;
but it was Robbish,
a private language if ever there was one,
everything in it made sense only through Rob and for Rob
    and in his, Rob's, perspective;
it became impossible to translate
and impossible to communicate with him.

Their common high school friend Andrea
who did crocheting as a hobby
still kept up contact with Rob,
but finally gave up too,
not excluding him actively,
but putting up a passive resistance.

And when put on the spot by Brenda
who assumed
    "knitting and crocheting, there must be common ground!"
Andrea said
    "Oh, no.
    It seems like it,
    but it's like German and Dutch

or math and physics
or Protestants and Catholics:
For outsiders it sounds very much like the same hogwash,
but they really don't get each other
and there's a lot of mutual resentment.
That's how it is between knitters and crocheters.
But his knitting *looks nice.*"
Andrea added this last part quickly
and Brenda acknowledged that
and they both expressed hope that Rob's engineering
    was going well too.

That evening, Brenda watched an old TV debate about sci-fi and
    religion she had on VHS
because lately, her vocabulary in those fields
    had been getting a bit rusty.

Brenda Craigdarroch
Felt It

Brenda Craigdarroch felt it when she saw her toothpaste spit disappear
   with the cold water in the sink.
She felt it when she heard the fridge go to sleep.
She felt it when she noticed the phone blinking at night.

She felt it when someone talked over the end credits of a movie.
She felt it when she saw printers
and dog sheds on sale
and tarps over cars.

She felt it once at an intersection
when she tried to see a raven, or just a crow,
landing on a tree in the distance,
but could not see it right because the traffic lights
and the electricity lines were in the way
and she was distracted by a good-looking guy in the car next to her.

There had been a time when she felt it when she saw Hallowe'en
   or Christmas decorations
in front yards
but that had passed — there were too many of those
and she did not feel it anymore when she saw them.

It was not that something was wrong
that you are angry and want to do something
like in politics

or that you are sad and blame someone
like in history.

It was not even that something was wrong —
rather, something was off.
It's like you're close to knowing something
but then something is in the way.

Brenda thought
it's like there's an obstacle which from one side looks like a signpost
but that's not quite it.
Brenda thought
it's like a revelation that you have no revelations
but that's not quite it.

One time she felt it when she looked out of a bus
and spotted that in one window
in one of the sixty or so houses that the bus passed on that street,
somebody had put up a picture of a lighthouse
and she wondered why anyone would put up a picture of a lighthouse
in their window
facing outwards
for whomever to see.

Then she vaguely remembered there was a picture
  in her childhood room
(that must have been in the apartment, before her parents moved
so she must have been less than four)
there was a picture of some radio tower on an island
and it emitted waves,
and she did not try to make a connection to that lighthouse,
she just thought: *waves.*
Brenda did not even imagine waves,
she just repeated the word to herself:
Waves.

Brenda felt it when she found bread in the cupboard
  that had turned into rock.

And she felt it one night
when she walked home alone from a party, slightly intoxicated
and by chance passed by her old high school
and saw that part of the building had been replaced
renovated
and all of it had been painted in different colours —
she felt it strongly then.

The only person she ever confided in
about feeling it
was her father.
She somehow suspected that he felt something similar
and at her next visit tried to describe it
and describe some situations where she felt it
and she saw he was welcoming that
and she got more confident and opened up about it
and then he said that he's not entirely sure if it's the exact same thing
but yes, he had felt it strongly
in his younger years actually.
Then for some decades, he said,
he had not felt it.
    "That was basically when we had you and while you grew up,
        Brenda,"
he said.
But he felt it again later
and now feels it quite often
ever since he lived alone, he said.

And Brenda asked
    "How would you describe it?"
And her father said
    "Well, at first I would say
        it's like seeing a seagull when you expect an eagle
        but that's not quite it.
        That's definitely not it
        but one can start from there
        and try to refine it, because it's not quite it.
        If somebody asked you

'Did you really expect an eagle?'
you'd have to honestly say no,
I had not actually expected an eagle.
Rather: Only after I saw the seagull
afterwards
in hindsight
a part of me thinks that I should have expected an eagle
   ...
But that's still not exactly it."

And Brenda said
  "That's close
    but it's still not it."

And they looked at each other
and they both felt it
right then
together.

Brenda Craigdarroch
and the Wasps

Imagine a country where it's normal to kick dogs.
Nobody in that country owns dogs,
but there are many stray dogs.
They are considered a pest
and it's socially acceptable to kick and beat them.

People sit in parks and have barbecues
   — nice people,
   normal people —
but when they see a dog from afar
they jump up and run after it
and try to kick it
or beat it with sticks.

Of course, the dogs don't like that.
Many of them just stay away from people,
but many fight and get ever more aggressive.

People love their food in that country
so in the summer they walk around
carrying sausages and steaks
and sticks — in case dogs come.

Some people say
maybe if you did not kick the dogs
they wouldn't be so aggressive,

maybe if you even gave them a piece of sausage
they would be happy and leave you alone.

But then everyone says that's crazy
and
    "Don't do that!
    These fuckers will just come back for more
    and even if *I* don't kick them
    probably somebody else gave them a good beating this morning
    so they will still be aggressive
    and by the way it's scientifically proven
    that dogs are aggressive by nature."
You say maybe some breeds
and they go
    "Yeah, whaddayawant?
    How'm I supposed to know what breed this fucker is?
    Sorry, there's children around here.
    We have to protect them —
    I know someone who was once bitten
    by a dog that had rabies."
And a dog comes, and they jump up and try to kick it.

And sometimes you hear an old lady
sitting in the park eating her hamburger,
and when a dog comes near, she fiddles with her walking stick
and yells
    "Oh, how I hate you darn *cats*!"

Imagine that country.

This is what Brenda Craigdarroch thought
every July and August
when she saw otherwise rational and mentally sane people
dealing with wasps.

In particular, that one day she sat on the patio
   of her favourite café and cake place
and overheard an old lady at another table saying

"Oh, those darn bees!
The restaurant should do something about them."

Brenda had a good imagination
but could not imagine how you can live 80 years
and not be able to distinguish bees from wasps
or cats from dogs.
She could just imagine that, if she approached her,
the lady would say
    "Oh, whatever. How would I know
    what four-legged furry creature that is?
    They both have teeth and claws, don't they?
    My friend got scratched by one of those dogs or cats recently —
    I don't want any of them near me."

Brenda always got angry in the summer.
and one day she discussed it with her friend, Manu
and figured out why she was angry.
It was not about the wasps.
    "Who gives a fuck about wasps?"
Brenda said.
It was about people being self-harmingly irrational
on cue.
You can be self-harmingly irrational by habit
due to some trauma
due to being tricked by commercials
due to fucked-up circumstances
but in this case people had just unconsciously learned to act weirdly
because everyone has always done it that way.
It just gets passed on from generation to generation:
little children see their parents running after dogs and kicking them
and think that's normal.
And everyone does it, the smart and the dumb —
suddenly they're all alike.

    "Sometimes that can be good,"
Manu said.
    "That's what makes society work.

If it just got unconsciously passed on from generation to generation
that you don't cheat
that you don't shoot,
if everyone knew that
if even the dumb and spiteful people somehow did that on cue
that would be great."
And Brenda just stared at him and said
    "I don't want to reform society,
    I just want people to stop being weird.
    No, I don't even want that anymore.
    I just want to be left in peace
    like the dogs
    or the wasps.
    It's not about the dogs.
    It's not about the wasps.
    Who gives a fuck about wasps?"
And then Brenda's voice dropped to a whisper.
    "It's about people doing it wrong
    and you just sit there and can do nothing about it
    and you'd given up trying to talk any of them out of it
        many a summer ago
    because you always got the same responses
    and so you've just accepted that you're
    one person in the park who is not
    hysterically waving and running and screaming.
    You just sit there
    in your black-and-yellow striped dress
    enjoying a summer day
    eating around the wasp on your apple
    silently watching
    and sometimes, some days, spotting someone else who is like you
    someone who quietly eats their sandwich and reads their book
    and with slow movements
    almost unconsciously
    avoids
    or carefully removes insects
    and if you notice each other, you just nod
    and hope for someday."

94

Brenda Craigdarroch
and the Glove

On one of her biweekly bicycle rides
from one side of town to the other
to stay overnight with her fourth boyfriend,
Brenda Craigdarroch lost one of her gloves.

She had been in a rush
and was already standing in the driveway
   with her bike and her gloves when she realized
that this Sunday was the first warm day of spring,
so instead of putting her gloves on her hands,
she crammed them into the front pocket of her sweater.

After about twenty minutes
of riding through annoying traffic,
there was a fast curve leading onto the trail
and when she leaned in there,
she heard what sounded like
a wet dishcloth hitting the counter,
looked around and saw one of her gloves had fallen out.
She stopped
and anxiously reached for her front pocket:
there was no other glove in there.
She knew the other one must have fallen out a while ago
and she felt bad.
She was late already and there was no point in turning back
and while she automatically picked up at least the one she saw now,

for a moment she considered
just leaving this one there on the street as well.

She had foreseen this when she had crammed them into her sweater:
She had foreseen that they would fall out.
Of course she had not actually foreseen it,
more like one of the three times a day when you think to yourself
    "This won't go well"
as a strange kind of psychological insurance
where, if things do turn out badly, you want to at least have the feeling
    that you saw it coming,
then in 80% of all cases, all goes well and you forget about it,
but in the remaining 20% you can say to yourself,
    "Fuck, I *knew* this would happen."

    "Fuck! I *knew* this would happen,"
Brenda shouted, to the surprise of some pedestrians,
and stuffed the one saved glove into her backpack.
The worst thing was that just a few months ago
    she had already lost a glove.
And the silliness of losing *one* glove,
turning the remaining glove into an utterly useless utensil
which just serves to remind you of your stupidity
and whose incompleteness becomes a symbol for
    the incompleteness of your life
and everything you're missing
and everything you have lost due to your own carelessness.

She could not tell her boyfriend about it.
She felt shame. She knew he would not actually care,
but *she* cared. It would be a nasty symbol: not for him, for her.
She did not want to share this.

She spent the rest of her bike ride partly telling herself
to not even try to come up with some silly excuse to ride back home at
    some point in the evening
and partly drafting and cross-checking such silly excuses.
But when she arrived,

her boyfriend was in an encompassingly good mood.
He had prepared a tofu risotto with white wine and capers,
which was delicious,
and afterwards he insisted on reading her a complete short story
    by Katherine Mansfield,
which was very tender,
and then they fooled around and had sex,
which was very tender,
and Brenda almost forgot about the glove in the course of
    all these activities.

The thought of it came back when she was lying awake after,
and then she almost told him about it,
but did not. She still wanted to keep it to herself, thinking,
    "That may be somewhat childish, but very natural."

The next morning, he drove her to her work, then went to his work,
and in the evening would pick her up again, like every Monday.
Luckily, the drive did not go along any of the roads where she had
    possibly lost the glove
so she was not tempted to stare through the window
or to ask him to drive slower or stop.

That Monday, Brenda finished work early
and walked back to her place.
Then she started to retrace her steps (or rather, her pedallings)
    along the streets
all the while bracing for the likely possibility the glove would be lost
as kind of a weird psychological insurance.
It was another warm day
and Brenda was not even sure what exact roads were between
    the suburban blocks she had taken.
She felt a bit desperate when she started walking up a hill
next to a busy street whose bike lane she definitely had taken,
knowing that after this hill, it would be only two more corners until the
    place she dropped the second glove,
and told herself again to brace for the possibility
    the first one would be lost,

thinking, it would be just a few bucks to get new gloves,
and now that it was getting warm
   she would not need gloves for some months anyway,
when she saw something black and small on the bike lane on the street.
She did not allow herself to start running,
   but kept walking up the hill slowly,
reasoning that most likely it was a piece of a tire
or another dead bird.
Coming closer, it looked like a glove.
It *was* a glove.
It was *her* glove.
It had been lying there on the asphalt, on the edge between the street
   and the bike lane for almost 24 hours.
She did resist taking a picture with her phone;
she extra-carefully walked onto the bike lane, checking for cars too,
   and picked it up.
It seemed to have some more scratches
but it was her glove.
She put it in her backpack with the other one,
walked home and texted her boyfriend
   to pick her up there in half an hour.

Notes

Brenda Craigdarroch
Never Believed Them
- "just a little too long"
cf. John Prine's first introduction to "The Other Side of Town" in a 2005 show as seen and heard on YouTube, and to be spoken the exact same way.
- "It is all not true!"
cf. A refrain of Nestroy's, "Und's is alles nicht wahr!", and what Karl Kraus refused to write about it.

Brenda Craigdarroch
Once Gave a Jigsaw Puzzle
- "the tree was cut down in a spiritual ceremony"
cf. "The Rebuilding of the Ise Shrine" in László Krasznahorkai's *Seiobo There Below*, called a novel in English, but a collection of stories in the German. The Hungarian original may defy description.

Brenda Craigdarroch
and the Philosophers
- "a taxonomic standard work of the same title, / but without definite article"
Mealybugs of California. With Taxonomy, Biology, and Control of North American Species (Homoptera, Coccoidea, Pseudococcidae) by Howard Lester McKenzie, University of California Press, 1967.

Brenda Craigdarroch
Would Not Stop Smoking
- "stuffed eggplant"
Μελιτζάνες παπουτσάκια.

- "gooseberry cream cake"
Stachelbeertorte.

- "Hagenbuch"
…through this author, has admitted now that these stories are strongly influenced by Hanns Dieter Hüsch's "Hagenbuch" stories, which in turn were heavily influenced by Thomas Bernhard's work, and where Bernhard got his ideas from, the devil knows.

This specific piece, however, would not exist were it not for a poem performed by Rachel McBride.

Brenda Craigdarroch's Keys
This story originated from crossing a recurring dream of the author's with a silly idea he had when looking at an office key with a very visible "Do Not Duplicate" on it. He still has the key, and the recurring dreams.

Brenda Craigdarroch
in Buenos Aires
- "does snow have corners"
- "the abstract concept of golf"
cf. Wittgenstein's *Philosophical Investigations* as well as Stewart Lee's stand-up routine "Office World Man".

Brenda Craigdarroch
and the Dishwasher
- "give it a playful punch"
cf. The Dubliners' song "The Button Pusher" and Rick Mercer's breakthrough play *Show Me the Button, I'll Push It*.

Brenda Craigdarroch
and Social Media
- "Top 10 Cartoon Shows from the 1970s Which Do Not Feature Dragons"
Apparently excluding Grisù, the

admirable dragon child who wants to become a firefighter.

Brenda Craigdarroch
    and Religions
• "temple, mosque, synagogue, church"
When reading this piece to a group of friends, it is advised to add the place where you usually meet them to the end of this list, like "or coffeehouse / football stadium / sacrificial centre". It will make them feel less lonely.

Brenda Craigdarroch
    and the Biocapacitator
• "biocapacitator"
A thorough Google search turns up *BioCapacitors — a novel category of biosensor*, described in vol. 24, issue 7 (March 2009), pp. 1837–1842 of the journal *Biosensors and Bioelectronics*; as well as *Biosupercapacitors*, described in vol. 5, issue 1 (2017), pp. 226–233 of the journal *Current Opinion in Electrochemistry*.

Whereas in the biocapacitor, "a biocatalyst, acting as a biological recognition element, oxidizes or reduces the analyte to generate electric power, which is then charged into a capacitor via a charge pump circuit (switched capacitor regulator) until the capacitors attains full capacity", thereas, "[i]n conventional biosupercapacitors the biomaterial serves as the pseudocapacitive component, while in self-charging biodevices the biocomponent also functions as the biocatalyst."

It is unclear to the author whether those two are related to each other. In any case, none of them is the device mentioned here.

Brenda Craigdarroch's
    Famous Raisin Cookies
• "famous raisin cookies"
    1 cup raisins
    ½ cup water
    ½ tsp baking soda
    1 cup sugar
    ½ cup butter
    ½ tsp vanilla
    1 large egg
    2 cups flour
    ½ tsp baking powder
    ¼ tsp salt
    ⅛ tsp nutmeg

Add hot water to raisins and cook briskly for five minutes. Cool, stir in soda. Let stand.

Cream butter and sugar until light. Add vanilla, beaten egg, cooled raisins and their liquid. Add flour with sifted spices. Stir.

Drop by spoonful on cookie sheet, leaving space for expansion. Bake 12 to 15 minutes at 175°C (347°F). Bake at 350°F at your own peril.

• "Death could stop Gogol and Dostoevsky from ruining sequels and writing shitty new *X-Files* episodes"
In a less upset state of mind, Brenda would concede that death is not the only thing which stopped Gogol and Dostoevsky from ever writing a single *X-Files* episode. Among the things which held them back, it features quite prominently though, especially in the case of Gogol.

• "obsessive footnotes"
...

BRENDA CRAIGDARROCH
    AND HER DENTIST
- "because you just stabbed them with a metal hook"

The author heard something along the lines of this line first from his friend Mark (unrelated to Brenda's acquaintance Marc in another story) and laughed out loud because he's had similar thoughts during dentist appointments for a while.

When preparing this story, he found that this joke has been turned into various memes for various years already (Google "dentist humour metal gums"), but he believes that the next line, about the eyeballs, is entirely owed to his own imagination.

BRENDA CRAIGDARROCH
    AND THE LAST PIECE OF ART
- "who all looked like Doug Ford"

An abridged version of this story was first printed in the anthology *The Last Piece of Art* (HuHuHu Press, Berlin 2019), for whose international audience "Doug Ford" was changed to "Donald Trump".

The author apologizes to all Canadians for thinking that few people outside of Canada would know who Doug Ford is, but he also thinks Canadians should be grateful for that.

BRENDA CRAIGDARROCH AND THE
    DEAD ROBIN IN THE GUTTER
- "shaggy cap mushroom plantation"

Coprinus comatus, the shaggy ink cap, lawyer's wig, or shaggy mane, is an edible mushroom which is never found in markets or shops because it's impossible to store: within hours after foraging, it turns into a disgusting ink-like liquid. Its flavour is not that outstanding either.

Such a plantation would be nonsensical from a purely economic point of view, like many other plantations.
- "that his e-bike dealer's cousin, who is an astronaut"

This story was related to the author by his friend Josh Vines, whose actual e-bike dealer's cousin is an actual astronaut, with photos of the rocket launch in Baikonur and the proud families and all. But not as an argument against conspiracy theories, just as a nice story. We tracked the ISS for a while too.

BRENDA CRAIGDARROCH
    TRIED HARD TO FORGET THINGS
- "It can be chasing pigeons in the park."

Not *poisoning* pigeons in the park, which would be plagiarism of a Tom Lehrer song. Only Georg Kreisler is allowed to plagiarize Tom Lehrer.

BRENDA CRAIGDARROCH'S
    CORRECT OPINIONS
- "and calf liver"

There is a niche on the internet where men who give advice on 'health', by which they mean white teeth and a bodybuilder physique, propagate liver as a 'superfood'. Weirdly, they eat it in the form of expensive, specially-ordered capsules, and not with onions.

BRENDA CRAIGDARROCH'S
    PREFERRED ZODIAC SIGN

The beginning of this piece wrote itself when Julia Day Flagg, friend of the author and ardent supporter of all things Brenda, shared a post on social media about how prescribing people a certain gender because of their sexual organs is not better than prescribing them a certain personality because of their birthdate.

- "…like those journalists who tried out waterboarding for themselves as if that makes them and their audience understand…"

cf. Köthe, Sebastian: "'Believe Me, It's Torture.' Reenactments von 'Waterboarding'" in *ffk Journal* (2019), Nr. 4, S. 85–97. DOI: https://doi.org/10.25969/mediarep/3707

BRENDA CRAIGDARROCH AND THE MONOLINGUAL PEOPLE

- "an old TV debate about Sci-Fi and religion she had on VHS"

In 1999, the Bavarian regional cultural TV station BR-alpha recorded a discussion between Linus Hauser, professor of theology, and Wolfgang Jeschke, one of the central figures in the German Sci-Fi scene, on this topic. The discussion was split into four episodes occasionally broadcast in the program's midnight–3 a.m. slot, between episodes of *The Joy of Painting with Bob Ross* and space footage set to ambient music.

At the end of each of the discussion fragments, the "Tears in Rain" closing theme from Vangelis' *Blade Runner* (the soundtrack to the film) was played, in a version without Roy's monologue, which became commercially available only a few years later on the 25th anniversary 3-CD box edition of said soundtrack. When they aired two of the episodes, they also played "Science-Fiction/Double Feature" from the *Rocky Horror Picture Show*.

It is totally unclear to the author how Brenda would have gotten wind of any of this.

BRENDA CRAIGDARROCH FELT IT

- "it's like a revelation that you have no revelations"

This is close to Borges' description of "el hecho estético" ("esta inminencia de una revelación, que no se produce", from his essay "La muralla y los libros"), but that's not quite it. Indeed, by an ultimately irrelevant causality chain, this text would not have been written without the 2019 CUPE strike in the Saanich School District SD63, and in spite of an odd nod to Virginia Woolf, it is the most accurate recording of sensations and thoughts on a long bike ride the author ever managed to put down in writing.

BRENDA CRAIGDARROCH AND THE WASPS

- "Manu"

Pronounced with stress on the first syllable, because it's the short form of Immanuel.

BRENDA CRAIGDARROCH AND THE GLOVE

- "Katherine Mansfield"
- "somewhat childish, but very natural": Katherine Mansfield's story "Something Childish But Very Natural" was first published in 1924 in the (posthumous) collection *Something Childish and Other Stories*. However, the story which Brenda's boyfriend read to her was either "Sun and Moon" or "Feuille d'Album" from the collection *Bliss and Other Stories*, first published in 1920.

About the Author

Born and raised in Germany, TORSTEN SCHOENEBERG published short stories there before immigrating to Victoria, BC in 2016, where he now teaches math at Camosun College and works at Russell Books.

Torsten keeps active in the regional poetry and literature scene of Vancouver Island, including as co-organizer of an open mic series, and has published poems in local publications such as *Oratorealis*.

Torsten lives in Victoria with his wife and daughter.